A Candlelight Ecstasy Romance

"ADAM, LISTEN TO ME—"

"No, Susannah, you listen to me. I made a legal agreement with your father to become a partner in the business. My copy was lost in the fire, and I don't know what happened to your father's copy. But as his heir you should honor his commitments." He stood and glared down at her. "I'm not sure you've believed me, even from the start. I'm not a liar, Susannah, no matter what you think!"

Susannah followed him to the front door, angry at the way the evening was ending. "Well, it sure is beginning to look as if *somebody* is!"

"So that's the way it is." Adam looked back at her, his eyes dark with misery. "You think *I'm* the liar, don't you?" When she didn't answer, he nodded slowly. "Thanks for everything. It was just great."

As the door slammed behind him, Susannah fought back her tears, wondering how she'd gotten into such a mess. . . .

CANDLELIGHT ECSTASY ROMANCES®

370 SO MUCH TO GIVE, *Sheila Paulos*
371 HAND IN HAND, *Edith Delatush*
372 NEVER LOVE A COWBOY, *Andrea St. John*
373 SUMMER STARS, *Alexis Hill Jordan*
374 GLITTERING PROMISES, *Anna Hudson*
375 TOKEN OF LOVE, *Joan Grove*
376 SOUTHERN FIRE, *Jo Calloway*
377 THE TROUBLE WITH MAGIC, *Megan Lane*
378 GOLDEN DAYS, *Kathy Clark*
379 LOVE IS ALL THAT MATTERS, *Tate McKenna*
380 FREE AND EASY, *Alison Tyler*
381 DEEP IN THE HEART, *Donna Kimel Vitek*
382 THAT SPECIAL SMILE, *Karen Whittenburg*
383 ALWAYS KEEP HIM LAUGHING, *Molly Katz*
384 A WHISPER AWAY, *Beverly Wilcox Hull*
385 ADD A DASH OF LOVE, *Barbara Andrews*
386 A STROKE OF GENIUS, *Helen Conrad*
387 THROUGH THE EYES OF LOVE, *Jo Calloway*
388 STRONGER THAN PASSION, *Emily Elliott*
389 THE CATCH OF THE SEASON, *Jackie Black*
390 MISTLETOE MAGIC, *Lynn Patrick*
391 POWER AND SEDUCTION, *Amii Lorin*
392 THE LOVE WAR, *Paula Hamilton*
393 EVENING THE SCORE, *Eleanor Woods*

AT LONG LAST LOVE

Andrea St. John

A CANDLELIGHT ECSTASY ROMANCE®

Published by
Dell Publishing Co., Inc.
1 Dag Hammarskjold Plaza
New York, New York 10017

For Johny, Shelli, Jarret, Andrew,
Sarah, and Susan—the most important
people in my life.

Copyright © 1986 by Don Howard

All rights reserved. No part of this book may be reproduced
or transmitted in any form or by any means, electronic or
mechanical, including photocopying, recording, or by any
information storage and retrieval system, without the written
permission of the Publisher, except where permitted by law.

Dell ® TM 681510, Dell Publishing Co., Inc.
Candlelight Ecstasy Romance®, 1,203,540, is a registered
trademark of Dell Publishing Co., Inc., New York, New York.

ISBN: 0-440-10405-X

Printed in the United States of America
First printing—January 1986

To Our Readers:

We have been delighted with your enthusiastic response to Candlelight Ecstasy Romances®, and we thank you for the interest you have shown in this exciting series.

In the upcoming months we will continue to present the distinctive sensuous love stories you have come to expect only from Ecstasy. We look forward to bringing you many more books from your favorite authors and also the very finest work from new authors of contemporary romantic fiction.

As always, we are striving to present the unique, absorbing love stories that you enjoy most—books that are more than ordinary romance. Your suggestions and comments are always welcome. Please write to us at the address below.

Sincerely,

The Editors
Candlelight Romances
1 Dag Hammarskjold Plaza
New York, New York 10017

CHAPTER ONE

Susannah Lockwood narrowed her dark-blue eyes, peering through the rain-streaked windshield of the rented Dodge Aries, then flicked on the turn signal. After checking the rearview mirror for traffic behind her, she swung into the parking lot adjacent to the modern, two-story building of brick and glass, hoping she'd found Lionel Morgan's new law offices. *This is it,* she thought, sighing with relief: there was Julia's Eldorado, parked a short distance from the other dozen or so cars occupying the parking lot.

She pulled into an empty slot next to her stepmother's Eldorado and switched off the ignition. For a moment she just sat there with her forehead resting against the cool top of the steering wheel, listening to the rain beating steadily on the roof of the small sedan—a lonely, desolate sound that perfectly suited her present mood.

"Oh, Dad," she whispered aloud, "why did it have to happen? Why?"

After a moment or two she drew a deep breath, lifted her chin, and adjusted the rearview mirror to check her appearance before joining the others inside. She pushed her short, naturally wavy brown hair away from her face with her hands, frowning at the sight of her shadowed, bloodshot eyes. She shook her head in exasperation as she took inventory of the familiar features looking back at her in the mirror: oval-shaped face with a firm, determined-looking chin; wide, generous mouth with a full lower lip; and small, nicely shaped nose. Her eyes—her best feature—were large, deep blue, and outlined by long, thick lashes. *It's not a bad face,* she reflected silently, *but—oh, to hell with it! I'm not here on a social occasion, and if anyone's displeased by my haggard, disheveled appearance, that's just tough! Let them spend seventy-two hours sitting around a snowed-in airport, and see how they look.*

With a last shake of her head she shoved the mirror back into place, picked up her purse, and opened the car door. She hurried toward the entrance of the impressive office building, chin held high in defiance of the chilly early January rain streaming from the dark southern California skies.

Inside the door she paused for a moment, shrugging out of her coat and looking around for a place to hang it. In one corner of the reception area, she saw a Christmas tree, the twinkling colored lights reminding her of two weeks before, when she'd spent Christmas with her dad and Julia before leaving for her vacation in Colorado.

"May I help you?" A bespectacled, perfectly coiffured young woman seated behind a large desk looked up from her typewriter, an inquiring expression on her face.

"I'm Susannah Lockwood. I'm looking for Lionel Morgan's office."

"Oh, yes, Miss Lockwood." The young woman came from behind the desk, reaching for Susannah's coat. "Let me take this for you. I'm afraid you're late for the reading of the will, but I think you'll find everyone just down the hall. They're serving coffee and tea in the library."

"Thank you."

Susannah walked down the hallway in the direction the woman had indicated, absently studying the new office building. The carpeting beneath her feet was thick and plush, and the paneled walls were hung with original oil paintings and expensive prints, all combining with soft, piped-in music and subdued lighting to create an ambience of wealth and dignity. *Altogether appropriate for one of the city of Upland's most distinguished private attorneys,* she mused.

She paused in the open doorway, listening to the low murmur of several conversations and scanning the crowd for familiar faces. On the far side of the room a polished rectory table had been set up, its surface covered with a large coffee urn and a dozen or so cups and saucers. Julia stood near the table, beckoning to her. Susannah smiled and began walking across the room, nodding and smiling woodenly at the half-familiar faces of distant relatives she saw only at weddings and funerals, smiling with a bit more sincerity at longtime employees of Lockwood Construction, whom she knew better and liked more. At the realization that these people had assembled to hear what her father had bequeathed to them, a trace of cynicism tinged her smile.

"Susannah, darling." Julia just looked at her for several seconds, then opened her arms. As they embraced, Susannah looked over her stepmother's shoulder and caught sight of Adam McBride, standing in a corner of the room and scowling at the cup of coffee in his large hand as if he were resisting the urge to smash it against the wall. Her breath caught as Adam looked up, but his pale-blue eyes swept across the room without seeming to recognize her.

He was even more handsome than the last time she'd seen him, which had been eight years ago at the end of summer when they had said their sweet good-byes and she had gone off to college. His face was leaner now, and his short, crisp, curly blond hair shone like spun gold under the artificial lighting. Broad shoulders stretched the fabric of his tan corduroy jacket, and a carelessly knotted dark-brown tie hung crookedly down the front of his white shirt, betraying the fact that he would have been more comfortable in a work shirt and jeans than in dress clothing. Many of the men here were more impressively dressed, Susannah reflected, but none could match him for sheer physical magnetism.

Adam McBride, she thought wonderingly, caught up

for a moment in bittersweet memories. Although Adam had now risen in the company to the position of one of the most trusted construction superintendents, when she had first met him he had been a laborer, only a year out of high school. He had actually started there part-time as a senior, but their paths had never crossed. When they finally met that fateful day, the attraction between the owner's daughter and the young, muscular laborer had been powerful and immediate, and when Adam had tentatively asked her out she had accepted with alacrity.

That had been the summer Susannah graduated from high school, and in the brief moment she gazed at Adam, she found herself reliving those halcyon, sun-drenched days. Long, lazy days at the beach; warm romantic evenings in Adam's battered old pickup truck, ignoring the action on the screen at the drive-in theaters in favor of the breathless excitement of discovering each other. They had become lovers that summer, and each of them had believed it would be forever.

Then reality had impinged on their romantic dreams. In September she went away to college to begin her studies for an engineering degree, whereas Adam continued to wield pick and shovel for her father's company. At first they had written often, making plans for the future, then, gradually, Adam's letters had tapered off and finally ceased altogether. Caught up in the pressures of study and social life at school, Susannah worried at first, then reluctantly resigned herself to the fact that she and Adam were simply not meant to be. When, during her final summer vacation between her junior and senior years, she heard that Adam had married, she tried to put him out of her mind once and for all.

Now, gazing across the room at him, she realized that she had failed . . .

"Oh, I'm so glad you're finally here," Julia said, snapping her back to the present. The two women parted, leaning back and gazing fondly at one another. "Did you have a good flight?"

"I don't even know, Julia." Susannah smiled wearily. "I tried to sleep through most of it. After almost three days of sitting around the airport, I was dead on my feet."

"Terrible way to have your vacation interrupted," Julia murmured soothingly, shaking her head in commiseration.

"When you told me about Dad, my vacation was the least of my worries," Susannah replied.

She'd been on her annual skiing vacation in Colorado when it happened. She had returned from a long day on the slopes to find Julia's telegram waiting for her at the lodge. She'd spent several hours attempting to place a call to California, but one of the worst blizzards in several years had knocked the telephone lines down, making it impossible to get through until the following morning. Then, after speaking to Julia, there had been another endless delay while she waited for the roads to be cleared so she could take a bus to the airport. All these factors, snow, isolation, and the remoteness of the skiing lodge, which she'd always considered a part of the charm of her winter vacations in Colorado, had conspired to prevent her from getting home in time to attend her father's funeral.

"The funeral was very nice," Julia began, as if replying to an unspoken question. "The Blackstones handled it for me. I never realized just how many friends Josh had in this town."

"Dad was very well liked. He—"

"Well, if it isn't the new owner of Lockwood Construction Company," a loud voice boomed in her ear, cutting her off. Susannah turned, an involuntary expression of irritation crossing her face at the sight of the tall, thin, bald-headed man who had spoken. "It's good to see you, Susie."

"Hello, Glen," she replied evenly. "How are you?"

Glen Vincent was the head accountant for Lockwood and although Susannah had known him since she was a small child she'd never really liked him. Vincent had always made a point of warning Joshua against taking his little girl tramping over various construction sites with him, pointing out the hazards to children that could be found there and reminding Josh that their insurance wouldn't cover Susannah if she were injured on one of the job sites. "It's no place for a little girl, Josh," Vincent would boom, and Susannah would cling more tightly to her father's hand and wish they could hurry away from this big man's threatening presence. She didn't understand the talk of insurance and liability and cancellations, but she understood that this man disapproved of her being with her father, and that was enough to engender a dislike for Glen Vincent that never subsided, even after she'd grown to adulthood.

"How am I indeed?" Vincent rumbled dryly, his smile vanishing. "Not as well off as I'd hoped to be today, I can tell you that. Fifteen years of faithful service apparently didn't mean as much to your father as it might have, Susie."

"Glen, for God's sake!" Julia's brown eyes blazed with fury as she faced her late husband's employee. "What kind of a remark is that? Have you lost your mind?"

Flushing, Vincent bowed briefly. "I apologize, Susie. Of course I—"

"My name is Susannah, if you don't mind."

"Ah, I see." Vincent stared at her for a moment, his eyes suddenly cold and speculative behind the lenses of his glasses. " 'Susannah,' then, or perhaps you would prefer 'Miss Lockwood,' in view of the fact that you are now apparently my employer?" He chuckled, but no trace of humor touched his eyes. "That is, if you're entertaining any thought of operating the company by yourself. A ridiculous idea, surely?"

"I don't know. I—I hadn't thought that far ahead." Susannah gestured vaguely. "I wasn't expecting . . ."

"Nobody was!" Vincent boomed, his good spirits apparently restored by her hesitation. "Now, then, Susannah, when you've had a chance to think things over a bit, I'd like to talk to you about the company. I've got a group of investors who just might be interested in taking the company off your hands—for a good price, of course," he added quickly, observing the expression on her face. Leaning forward, he lowered his voice. "I *think* I can get you as much as two hundred grand for your equity—maybe as much as a quarter of a mil. Just between you and me, you'd be a fool to pass up an offer like that."

"She'd be a fool if she took it, Vincent," a low, baritone voice interjected. Susannah felt a thrill of recognition at the sound of that voice. She turned, and Adam McBride nodded briefly to her, then directed a hostile glare at Glen Vincent.

"You're just too damned generous for your own good, aren't you? Especially since a nice piece of the company would wind up in *your* pocket if she agreed, wouldn't it? Just back off, you and the rest of your vultures! Hell, the tool inventory alone is worth more than your offer!"

"In the case of a distress sale—" Vincent sputtered, but Adam cut him off with a chopping gesture.

"Distress sale? Nobody knows what's going to happen at this point, Glen. Give the lady a chance to catch her breath before you start pressing, okay?" Pausing, Adam drew a deep, ragged breath. "But I can tell you this much: an auction would bring more than your offer, just for the tools and equipment, so you can tell your partners that Susannah didn't just fall off the turnip truck."

Glen Vincent swallowed, his face a deep crimson as he glared at the three of them, Susannah, Julia, and Adam. Abruptly, he nodded, a malevolent gleam in his eyes. "You just think it over, Susannah. It would be a mistake—a *big* mistake—for you to try to run the company yourself." Before she could reply, he nodded again, then turned on his heel and stalked away.

"The *nerve* of that bastard!" Julia muttered furiously, tears of rage shining in her eyes as she faced Susannah. Pausing, she gradually regained control of herself, then smiled weakly at Adam. "Thanks for putting him straight, Adam."

"Yes, thank you," Susannah added. She passed a hand across her eyes, suddenly weary beyond words. The ugly confrontation had left her drained, and on top of the grief, confusion, and frustration of the past few days, it had been just about enough to knock her off her feet. "It's good to see you, Adam," she murmured.

His blue eyes softened as he looked at her. "And it's good to see you, Susannah," he said quietly. He made an awkward gesture. "Sorry about that outburst with Vincent, but I just couldn't keep my mouth shut when I heard what he was up to. These things have a way of bringing out the very worst in people, it seems." He hesitated for a moment, a troubled expression crossing his face, then said, "Which makes it all the harder to say what I have to, but—"

"Adam, can't it wait?" Julia interrupted. She smiled at her stepdaughter as she took her arm. "I think I'd better get this young lady home before she collapses on the spot. It's been days since she's had any rest. You understand, don't you?"

"Of course," Adam replied quickly. He touched Susannah on the shoulder, and despite her weariness, a little shiver coursed through her body at the contact. "I'll call you soon, if I may?"

"Yes, I'd like that, Adam."

He stared at her for another moment, then nodded and walked away, working his way through the crowded room toward the exit. As he vanished through the door, Susannah sighed and turned to Julia.

"I wonder what's on his mind?"

"Well, whatever it is, it can wait," Julia stated firmly. "Let's get out of here. I've had about all of this I can stand myself. You can ride home with me."

"But I've got a rental car," Susannah protested as Julia began leading her from the room. "And all my luggage—"

"Don't worry about a thing," Julia assured her. Stopping next to a familiar-looking couple on the fringes of a larger group, she tapped the man on his shoulder. He turned and nodded, smiling solicitously at Susannah, and she recognized Ralph Whitman, one of the foremen who had worked for Lockwood and Sons for many years.

"Ralph, would you be kind enough to drive Susannah's rental car over to the house for me and drop her stuff off before returning it to the airport?" Julia asked.

"Sure, no problem. Good to see you, Susannah. I hear you're a big-time civil engineer these days. Congratulations." His weathered face became solemn as he remembered the occasion. "We're all real sorry about the old ma— about your father, I mean."

"Thanks, Ralph." Susannah smiled understandingly. "We're all going to miss him."

After turning over the keys to the rented car, she followed Julia through the crowded room toward the exit. After retrieving their coats in the reception area, they walked out of the building together, grateful for the cool, fresh air after the stuffy closeness of the room full of people. The rain had stopped now, Susannah observed, but the gray, damp afternoon air had a penetrating chill that seemed, in its own way, even more uncomfortable than the crisp, dry cold of Colorado. She shivered as she picked her way around the puddles that had formed in the parking lot, following Julia toward the cream-colored Eldorado that had been her fortieth birthday present from Josh just last summer.

Susannah sank gratefully into the plush leather cushions as Julia started the engine and backed out of the parking space. Now that the ordeal of the meeting in Lionel Morgan's office was over, the accumulated weariness of the last few days seemed to be gathering in her bones, dragging her toward a numb state of semiconsciousness. Resisting the seductive pull toward sleep, she sat up straighter, looking out through the windows at the passing landscape.

"Not another shopping center!" she exclaimed, as the car halted at a traffic light. The last time Susannah had been by this area, the space now occupied by a small shopping center had been filled by a lovely grove of avocado trees, row upon row of the lush, green trees covering several acres. "I guess they won't be happy until the whole darned state is paved over."

"Smile when you say that," Julia remarked wryly. "As the owner of a construction company now, you're hardly one to complain about developments."

Susannah nodded, a wistful expression on her face. "When I was in school, this whole area in through here was covered by orange and lemon groves. Just look at it now. Fast-food joints, liquor stores, and supermarkets, all of it still decked out with tinsel and colored Christmas lights."

"I know," Julia said. "Christmas never seems quite real to me, here in southern California. When I was a girl, growing up in Colorado, it was somehow magical . . ."

Susannah reached over and touched Julia on the shoulder.

"If I didn't have anything else to thank you for, Julia, introducing me to Colorado and teaching me to ski would be more than enough to earn my eternal gratitude."

"But you weren't so sure about me when Josh first brought me home to meet you, were you?" Julia asked with a fond smile.

"Oh, Julia, I was fourteen! What did you expect? Mom died when I was twelve, and Dad brought home a replacement I was supposed to welcome with open arms?" She paused a moment, continuing after the light had changed and Julia had accelerated the big car. "I must have seemed like a terrible little brat to you in those days, but you knew how to handle me, right from the start."

"You were *not* a brat," Julia declared. "You were a lonely little girl who needed the help and advice of an older woman to get through a difficult time in your life. I was able to be that for you, but I would never have even tried to replace your mother. Nobody could have done that."

"So we became friends instead," Susannah added pensively. "And you've always been a wonderful friend, Julia. I want you to know that."

Julia looked away for a moment, but not before Susannah saw the quick gleam of tears in her eyes. "We did make it work, didn't we? We were a pretty happy family, all things considered." She paused a moment, shaking her head and smiling. "You know, every Christmas I'm reminded of that first year you were in college, when you and Josh sat around on Christmas Eve playing those old Jimmy Dorsey and Glenn Miller albums while I groaned and held my ears . . . Want to know something? I like that kind of music, too, but I always pretended not to, to give you and Josh something special to share between the two of you. Which reminds me—Josh left his record collection to you."

"Oh, but I couldn't take it," Susannah protested. "Not now, now that I know you like the music, too."

"Don't worry about it," Julia said, waving her objections away. "I've got most of them taped . . . By the way I have a copy of the will. You can look it over when you want to. I'm sure Morgan will mail you a copy, but in the meantime you can look mine over."

Nodding distractedly, Susannah gazed out through the windows of the car. They were passing through residential neighborhoods now, so they were almost home. *Home.* Even though she hadn't lived in Upland for several years, since graduating from college and accepting a position as a civil engineer for the U.S. Navy in San Diego, she still thought of the house here as her real home. And as they approached her childhood home, the loss of her father suddenly became much more real to her; the realization that she would soon be there, surrounded by his things, pierced her with a sudden agony that she had been able to fend off until now.

"Julia, how did it happen?"

Julia glanced sharply at her, hesitating briefly before

replying, as if wondering how much of the truth her stepdaughter was able to handle. She flicked on the turn signal, then turned onto the familiar street. As she guided the big car into the driveway and stopped before the wide garage door, she turned to face Susannah.

"Well, it's kind of strange, really," she began faintly. "I still haven't figured it out in my own mind . . . Josh drove up into the San Gabriel Canyon to look over the site of a big job he was bidding on. On the way back, evidently, he—he just drove off the highway, over a sheer cliff of nearly two hundred feet. They—the police—think he must have been drunk." She paused, looking away as she removed the keys from the ignition. With her hand on the door handle she continued, almost inaudibly, "Susannah, there were no skid marks."

CHAPTER TWO

No skid marks.

The instant Susannah opened her eyes, Julia's words sprang into her mind. She pushed the thought away, unwilling to face the implications it created. For now, it was enough just to deal with the grief caused by her father's death. Two weeks ago, they had spent Christmas together. Although her father had seemed distracted, he had been alive. And now . . .

The beauty of the day seemed to mock her as she lay in the familiar bed in the home in which she had grown to young womanhood. Buttery gold sunlight streamed through the lacy curtains, filling the room with warmth and cheer in direct counterpoint to her mood. With a sigh she sat up on the edge of the bed, noting that her luggage had been delivered to her room sometime during the night. At least she would be able to change her clothes.

Her thoughts were filled with flashbacks of the day before. Her apprehension of yesterday afternoon had been well founded: the moment she'd set foot in the house, the death of her father had become intensely, painfully real to her, and the grief she'd been blocking since receiving the telegram in Colorado could no longer be denied. Pleading exhaustion, she'd excused herself from Julia and fled to her room. There, she'd given free rein to the tears she'd been bottling up for too long, falling into an exhausted, dreamless sleep after an hour or more of nonstop weeping.

"Stop it," she told herself now, dabbing at the corners

of her eyes. "He's gone, and all the tears in the world won't bring him back. And if he *did* drive off that cliff deliberately, it's up to me to find out *why*."

Twenty minutes later, after a refreshing hot shower, dressed in soft, faded jeans and a loose pullover sweater, she joined Julia in the large family room adjacent to the kitchen.

"Morning. Did you sleep well?" Julia was seated at the dining room table in the center of the family room, a cup of coffee in front of her. As always she was immaculately made up, and her blond hair looked as if she had just come from a visit to the hairdresser's salon. From the overflowing ashtray on the table in front of her, it was apparent that she'd been sitting there for at least an hour.

"Mmm. I was exhausted." Pouring coffee from the pot on the breakfast bar, Susannah carried the mug over to the sliding glass door that led out to the patio. She slid the door open with one hand, holding the coffee mug carefully with the other, and inhaled deeply. The air was fresh, crystal clear, and just cool enough to make her grateful for the pullover. "When did you start smoking again, Julia?"

"Oh, you know." Julia shrugged as she put out her latest cigarette, adding it to the heap in the ashtray. "All the stress, the company . . . everyone sitting around filling the house up with smoke. What can I say? I'm weak, kid."

Getting up from the table, she walked around the breakfast bar, which separated the kitchen from the family room, and peered into the refrigerator. "Hungry? Can I fix you some breakfast? Jennie Whitman brought over a great honey-cured ham."

"I'm famished," Susannah admitted. "Ham and eggs would be great." She walked out onto the patio, looking toward the San Gabriel Mountains. Just a few miles to the north, Old Baldy, its soft round top covered with snow, was etched clearly against a bright, almost impossibly blue sky. "What a beautiful day," she murmured.

"Isn't it, though?" Julia agreed, looking over at the open door. " 'Chamber of commerce weather,' Josh always called days like this . . ." She rummaged in the refrigerator for a moment, finally emerging with a carton of eggs. "How do you want your eggs?"

"Here, let me help with that." Susannah hurried back inside the house, sliding the door shut behind her. For the next half hour the two women were occupied with preparing and consuming a large breakfast, and conversation was at a minimum.

After the breakfast dishes had been rinsed and stacked in the dishwasher, they refilled their coffee mugs and sat back down at the table. Julia lit a fresh cigarette and inhaled deeply, squinting at Susannah through a gray haze as she exhaled.

"What are your plans, honey? Are you going back to San Diego, or will you live up here for a while? You know that you're welcome to stay in your old room for as long as you like. I'd love to have you here."

"Oh, I'll have to go back, no matter what I decide about the future. There's my job to think of, and my apartment . . ." She paused, sipping at the coffee, then leaned forward, resting her chin on her hand as she gazed at Julia. "How about you? What are you going to do?"

"Oh, I don't know. I guess I'll have to do *something*." Julia grinned sourly. "Though I'm a little long in the tooth to go back to Vegas and dance, which is just about my only marketable skill, I suppose."

"It's none of my business, but how did Dad leave you?"

"Oh, fine, just fine." Julia puffed quickly on the cigarette, then stabbed it out with a look of disgust. "This place will automatically be paid off with the mortgage insurance. And Josh was heavily insured. There's no financial reason for me to work, but I think I'd probably go bananas if I just sat around getting fat." She gave a harsh laugh. "I'd probably wind up getting sloshed at the club every afternoon, until you had to have me put away somewhere. I'll find something useful to do . . ." She looked around the large room for a moment, then took a deep breath and got to her feet, picking up the ashtray and carrying it over to the trash receptacle.

"But first I'm going to give this old barn a good cleaning. Ever since last Saturday this house has been full of people coming and going, just sitting around getting in the way. I know they were all trying to help and comfort me, but they *did* create a mess."

Susannah thought for a moment. There was no pressing need for her to do anything, to decide anything. Her vacation didn't end until the third week in January. There was plenty of time for necessary decisions before then. "I'll help you," she said impulsively. "I could use a good workout."

"Great." Julia beamed at her, her hands on her slender hips. "It'll be just like old times."

Enthusiastically the two women began in the back of the large, sprawling, ranch-style house, working their way through the bedrooms with vacuum cleaner, furniture polish, and stacks of fresh linen and towels. Susannah enjoyed the physical activity after the enforced idleness of the past several days. She and Julia paused occasionally to grin at each other, savoring the camaraderie they shared.

When Susannah was vacuuming the carpet in the living room, she paused at the Christmas tree for a moment, experiencing a fresh pang of grief as she remembered how they had sat around opening their gifts on Christmas morning. She resolutely turned away and continued her work, refusing to think about the sting of tears she felt in her eyes.

By the time they stopped at one o'clock that afternoon, the house was gleaming like a new penny, and if it hadn't been for the mound of soiled bedding and bath towels waiting to be laundered, the work would have been complete.

"To hell with the washing," Julia declared grandiosely, with a broad gesture. "It'll keep for a few days."

She smiled as she blew a wisp of disarrayed blond hair away from her mouth. "I feel pretty darned good. How about you?"

Susannah returned her smile, nodding in agreement. "Ready for a bite of lunch?"

"I don't think so, after that breakfast. But you go ahead."

"I probably shouldn't, but that honey-cured ham's calling me." As Julia started toward the kitchen, the telephone rang. "It's for you," she called, after picking up the receiver.

Susannah took the phone, hoping it wasn't a sympathy call. Her heart skipped a beat at the familiar sound of the low baritone voice.

"Susannah, this is Adam. I'd really like to talk to you, if you're not busy this afternoon. How about lunch?"

She paused, uncertain as to how to respond. Adam was a married man, she reminded herself, and no matter what they had once been to each other, all that was in the past now. On the other hand, if this *was* strictly a business call, as he had intimated yesterday in Lionel Morgan's office, it would be foolish and impolite to refuse.

"Listen," he broke in impatiently, as if he'd been reading her mind, "I'm asking you to have lunch with me, not to go out on a date. It's important, Susannah."

"All right," she agreed, making up her mind, "but give me an hour. I've been cleaning house all morning, and I'm a mess."

"Fine. I'll pick you up at two."

Susannah slowly replaced the receiver, a troubled expression on her face. It occurred to her that she was going to have to make a conscious effort to avoid Adam McBride in the future if just hearing his voice had this effect on her. She felt Julia staring at her from the breakfast bar and turned to give her an embarrassed little shrug.

"Was that Adam McBride?"

"Yes. We're going to lunch."

23

"I thought I recognized his voice." Julia raised her eyebrow. "You and he were quite an item at one time, weren't you?"

"I was crazy about him, Julia," she admitted after a moment. She walked over and sat down at the breakfast bar next to Julia. "But that was a long time ago. Things change . . ."

"Uh-huh," Julia said, eyeing her skeptically. "You knew he lost his wife a couple of years ago, didn't you?"

"No!" Susannah exclaimed.

"I thought Josh told you about it." Julia sliced off a slab of ham and placed it on whole wheat bread. "It was a fire. They were living in a mobile home, and Adam was out of town on a job when it happened."

"How terrible! It must have been awful for him." Susannah wondered why her father had never mentioned the tragedy to her. Surely he remembered that she and Adam had once been close . . . *Perhaps he'd wanted to spare me*, she thought.

"It happened that summer you went to the Caribbean," Julia said, frowning. "We didn't see you until Christmas that year, and by then it was old news." She glanced sideways at Susannah as she took a bite of her sandwich. "Anyway, if memory serves me, Josh always avoided the subject of Adam McBride whenever you were around."

"Yes, well . . ." Susannah slid off her stool and walked toward her bedroom, filled with conflicting emotions. While she felt sorrow for Adam's tragic loss, part of her couldn't help reflecting that as a widower he was, however distantly, available. "I guess I'd better have another shower if I'm going out to lunch."

When the doorbell chimed at two, Susannah hurried to open the door. She had carefully dressed in new designer jeans, low heels, and a pale rose sweater. A dark-blue silk scarf was knotted loosely around her throat, and her dark-blue eyes were shining with anticipation as she reached for the door knob.

"Hello, Susannah." Adam smiled, his even white teeth flashing in his tanned face.

"Hi, Adam. Come in for a minute?"

"Sure." He followed her into the family room, where Julia was seated at the table. She looked up from the newspaper she'd been reading and smiled as Adam greeted her.

"Hi, Adam. You're looking well."

Susannah inspected him as he stood in the doorway between the family room and living room, seeming to fill it to the limit. He was dressed in a white turtleneck sweater and a pair of tan, tight-fitting slacks that emphasized the smooth curves of his leg muscles. With his shining gold hair, blue eyes, and dazzling white teeth, he presented an image of masculine appeal that took Susannah's breath away.

His eyes crinkled in a good-natured smile at Julia's compliment. "Thanks. You're looking good, too." He turned to Susannah. "You ready?"

As they left through the front door, Susannah smiled as she caught sight of Adam's vehicle. He no longer drove a battered old pickup, but it *was* a pickup—a new GMC crew cab model with big dual rear tires. Adam opened the door for her, and she climbed in, observing that the plush velour upholstery inside was nicer than many cars.

"Still driving pickups, I see," she kidded as he got in under the wheel and started the engine.

"Oh, sure." He smiled as he pulled smoothly away from the curb. "I need a truck in my line of work. This thing rides like a car, but it's got four-wheel drive, and it'll go almost anywhere a Jeep will." He glanced over at her as he stopped at the intersection at the end of the block. "You're sure looking good, Susie."

"Thank you, Adam." She looked at him, a spark of mischief in her eyes. "I'm not sure I should return the compliment. I'm sure you hear it often enough."

He gave a self-deprecating grin. "How hungry are you? A little bit, medium, or starved? I know a great

Mexican place where they make terrific margaritas, and they really feed you."

"Oh, a little bit, I guess." As his face fell, she quickly added, "But I could just have a taco or something, if you'd really like to go there."

"Good. That's it, then."

In spite of the heavy traffic, it took less than ten minutes to get to the restaurant. Susannah observed that others cars seemed to yield willingly to Adam's large pickup. After parking, Adam hurried around to open the door for her, then led her inside, his hand protectively on the small of her back.

The interior of the restaurant was decorated with bricked arches and fake adobe walls. Sombreros, guitars, and tambourines were hung here and there, lending what the owners obviously hoped was the ambience of old Mexico. Adam noticed her surreptitious inspection and smiled.

"I know it's a little overdone, but the food really *is* terrific."

The hostess, dressed in a colorful peasant blouse and a swirling Mexican skirt, led them to a padded banquette with a candle flickering on the table. Adam stood while Susannah seated herself, then ordered two margarita *grandes* as he sat down.

"*Grandes?* That sounds pretty ominous, Adam," she protested. "Maybe I'd better just have a single. I'd hate to make a fool out of myself over lunch."

"Oh, you couldn't do that," he assured her with a confidence she was far from feeling. "You're one of the most levelheaded people I've ever known."

She thought she detected a note of irony in his voice and glanced sharply at him, but his expression revealed nothing of his feelings.

They sat in silence until the drinks arrived, Susannah studying the other diners and wondering what was on Adam's mind.

"Would you like to wait a few minutes before ordering?" the waitress asked as she placed the drinks on the table.

"That will be fine." Adam smiled as Susannah stared at the large glass, flakes of salt sticking to the rim. As she picked it up, he reached out with his own, clicking the rims together in a toast. "Well, here's to the new owner of Lockwood and Sons."

"Thank you." She sipped at the drink, feeling the warm tingle from the tequila radiating out from the pit of her stomach. As he had promised, the drink was delicious, but it was also potent. *One of these,* she thought, *will be enough.* "What was it you wanted to discuss with me, Adam?"

"All business, huh?"

She felt a little tingle as his pale-blue eyes met hers and resisted the impulse to take a gulp of her drink. Just being in his presence after all these years was intoxicating enough, without fanning the flames with alcohol.

"Couldn't we just be sociable for a few minutes? Catch up on old times?"

She smiled fondly into his eyes. "We *did* have some fun, didn't we?" As he returned her smile, she wondered about the wisdom of looking back. Nostalgia was almost painfully sweet at times, but she realized that it could also be dangerous.

"That we did, lady, that we did." He raised his glass and took a sip, his eyes never leaving hers. "I'll never forget those all-night beach parties, just the two of us under the stars . . . listening to the pounding of the surf."

And the pounding of our hearts beating together, she remembered, *as we discovered the wonder of each other.*

She smiled, caught up in the memories. "Remember the fat cop that one time?" She giggled, a mischievous glint in her eyes. "I think he was more embarrassed than we were."

"Yeah." Adam grinned, his white teeth sparkling in the dim lighting. "I thought he was going to swallow that flashlight of his." He shook his head slowly. "Oh, Susie, those were some good times, weren't they?" He reached across the table and patted the back of her hand. Alarm bells began to jangle in her mind. She jerked her hand away.

"Maybe we'd better get back to the present," she suggested quickly, raising her glass and taking a drink.

"Sure," he said, his eyes turning cool as he pulled back his hand. "A lot of water has gone under the bridge since we were kids, Susie. We've both changed." His lips twisted as he asked, "Are you afraid to look back?"

"Oh, I've looked back plenty of times. But the past was painful enough when I was living it." Throwing caution to the winds, she raised her glass and took a large gulp, feeling the warmth of the alcohol spreading through her stomach. "I'd rather look to the future, if you don't mind."

"I see," he replied. "You'd just as soon forget that you and I were ever anything but employ*ee* and employ*er*, is that it? Well, don't worry, lady—I got the message a long time ago, when you broke it off with me."

"*I* broke it off? You were the one who stopped writing! And unless my memory deceives me, you were also the one who got married while I was still in school."

He lowered his eyes, but not before she saw the hurt in them. "I married a girl who didn't think she was above me." He snorted bitterly. "A common laborer, with no prospects for the future . . . Sure, I stopped writing. I was afraid I wasn't really good enough for you, and you were just too kind to tell me to my face. And when you didn't write, or call, or come around when you were home, I knew I was right."

Susannah took a sip of her margarita, avoiding his eyes. Was there an element of truth in his words? Looking back on those days now, from the perspective of more than five years, she realized she could not flatly deny his accusation. Yes, she *had* been caught up in her studies and social life at school, but had there been moments when she questioned her judgment in continuing a relationship with an ordinary laborer when she was going to become an engineer? *What arrogance,* she thought wonderingly. To equate a college education with intelligence, ambition, and drive while denying that lesser-educated individuals could possess those same attributes now seemed arrogant beyond belief.

"So you were testing me when you stopped writing," she said.

"Maybe." He looked moodily into his drink. "I guess my self-esteem wasn't all that high in those days. But I figured if you loved me enough, you wouldn't give up on us without a fight."

"Oh, Adam, what can I say? I was a lot younger then and pretty stupid in lots of ways. If I ever felt better than you, I was wrong." She reached across the table and patted his large, calloused hand. He caught her hand and squeezed it before releasing it, sending a shiver of pleasure up the length of her arm.

"Besides," she continued, "by any standard anybody would care to use, you're more of a success than I am. You're not thirty yet, and you're one of the company's most valued superintendents, out in the field doing exciting things, seeing projects through from start to finish. Me? I'm a junior civil engineer, sitting in a boring office shuffling papers like any other bureaucrat. And I'm sure you must earn at least twice the money I do."

"Maybe that *was* true," he admitted, "but no more. Now you own the whole damned company, and I'm just a salaried employee. Back where we started, right?" With a mocking little smile he raised his glass, toasting her again before he took a sip. "Which brings me around to the reason I wanted this little talk, Susannah . . . God, there's just no easy way to say this. Three years ago, your father promised to make me a partner in the company on my tenth anniversary with the company. He drew up a formal agreement, and we both signed it and had it notarized." He paused a moment, then looked into her eyes. "Susannah, my tenth anniversary with the company will be this March, about two months from now."

"You—you're saying that you'll become part owner of the company? This March?"

"On March fifteenth," he declared, "twenty-five percent of the company." After a few seconds he lowered his eyes, as if embarrassed by her disbelieving expression. "Josh didn't think you'd ever want to run the company, especially since you had such a good job and all, and . . . well . . . I hate to put it like this, but he often said that he sort of looked on me as—as the son he never had."

"This is . . . incredible," she managed at last, sagging back against the seat of the banquette. "You say that Dad was simply going to *give* you twenty-five percent of his company? Why wasn't it mentioned in the will?"

He shook his head, a troubled expression on his face. "I don't know. I just don't know. It's not as crazy as it probably sounds to you. During the past couple of years I've been practically running the company anyway. Josh was having less and less to do with the everyday operation." He paused, the frown growing deeper as he continued. "And then, during the past six months, he practically stopped coming in at all. I'd been really worried, Susannah. He hadn't been himself in a long time."

"He seemed quiet when I saw him at Christmas, but . . . Julia didn't mention any of this," she said softly, struggling against a growing feeling of disbelief. "Are you sure, Adam?"

His mouth flattened into a hard, thin line. "I'll stand still for a lot, Susannah, but I'm *not* a liar."

"Oh, I didn't mean to imply that you were lying. It's just—just such a surprise, that's all." She fell silent, her thoughts in a turmoil as she tried to reconcile the image Adam had painted of her father with the one she remembered so clearly. Josh had devoted a lot of time to his company. It seemed almost impossible that such drastic changes could have occurred in such a short amount of time.

Briefly she considered telling Adam what Julia had told her, that there had been no skid marks at the scene of Josh's fatal accident. After a moment she decided to keep the information to herself—at least for the time being.

"Well, anyway, I guess this kind of puts the ball in your court," Adam said, breaking the silence.

"What's that?"

"Will you honor the agreement I had with Josh?" he asked patiently.

"Oh. Well, I—of course I will. If you had a legal agreement with Dad, I'll honor it. He wouldn't have made such an agreement if he didn't intend to honor it." She paused for a moment, then nodded decisively. "Just let me have a copy of the agreement to show to Lionel Morgan, and if it's what you say it is, we'll have the papers drawn up right away."

Adam's tanned face darkened with embarrassment. "Well, that's going to be a problem. My copy of the agreement is gone, and I don't have any idea what Josh did with his. That's why I was hoping there'd be something in the will."

"Gone?" She stared incredulously. "Adam, how could you lose something so important?"

"It was unavoidable," he muttered.

"Unavoidable? You seem to have a pretty casual attitude toward things that are important!"

"It went up in the fire," he choked out, his eyes squeezed almost shut. His fist pounded the table. "Dammit, it wasn't *my* fault!"

Susannah felt like weeping from shame. She ducked her head to avoid his eyes while she tried to compose herself.

"Adam, I'm sorry," she whispered. "Julia just told me about the fire this morning. I'm so sorry about your wife. Of course it couldn't have been your fault."

"At least I still have Sheila," he said after a moment.

He drank deeply from his glass. "One of the neighbors managed to get her out, thank God." He paused a moment, then muttered almost inaudibly, "It *wasn't* my fault."

"Sheila?" Susannah frowned, wondering what was behind his fear that he would somehow be blamed for the fire that destroyed his home and killed his wife. "Who's Sheila?"

"My daughter." He looked up at her, his eyes moist and filled with a father's love. "She just turned three last month. I tell you, Susie, she's changed my life. I never realized how much being a father could change the way a guy looks at things. When I look at her . . . I see myself, and I see Ann . . . I get just a little glimmer of understanding of what life is all about." He paused and took a deep breath. "She's what kept me going during those first few months after the fire . . ."

She looked at him in silence for a moment. He was right: they *had* changed. Adam had matured, become stronger, more self-reliant. And at the same time, being a father had made him vulnerable in a way that he had never been before. For a moment she envied him; being a parent had changed him for the better, and this was an experience that still lay in her future. It was as if he were party to a secret she could still only guess at. She smiled, liking this new Adam even more than the one she remembered. Cockiness had been replaced by self-confidence; his devil-may-care attitude by a sense of responsibility toward his daughter. She had fallen in love with a boy, but this was a man seated across the table from her.

"So you see," he said quietly, "I have to think of my daughter's future now."

"Of course you do." She looked at him for a moment, then made up her mind. "Adam, I'll look for Dad's copy of the agreement. He must have filed it somewhere. If I can find it, I'll honor it. Fair enough?"

He studied her for a moment, then nodded. "Fair enough, I guess." Sighing, he pushed himself back from the table. "Are you hungry, Susie? I've kind of lost my appetite."

"Me, too," she agreed. "Let's go."

As they pulled away from the parking lot in his pickup, Adam looked over at her. "Susannah, I'd appreciate it if you didn't waste any time in locating Josh's copy of that agreement, okay?"

"Well, sure, but what's the hurry?" she asked.

"It's just that I'd like to get it all cleared up as soon as possible, before you—before you sell the company. The new owners might not be as fair-minded as you about honoring such an agreement."

"The new owners?" She stared at him. "Who said anything about selling the company? I haven't made up my mind what I'm going to do yet."

"Well," he said with a slight laugh, "what choice do you have?" When she didn't reply at once, his eyebrows shot up until he was gaping at her incredulously. "Hey, you're not thinking of trying to operate the company on your own, are you?"

"And why not?"

"Why not?" His eyebrows drew down into a fierce scowl. "Because it's a damned ridiculous idea, that's why! Whoever heard of a woman trying to run a construction company?"

"If nobody ever heard of such a 'ridiculous idea,'" she returned coolly, twisting around in her seat in order to stare directly into his face, "then maybe it's an idea that's long overdue."

33

CHAPTER THREE

Susannah walked out onto the patio Monday morning, a cup of coffee in her hand, and looked up toward the mountains. Mount Baldy was concealed by the low-hanging, lead-colored clouds over the valley, and the air was ripe with the promise of rain. Shivering slightly from the damp air, she walked back inside the house, pulling the sliding door shut behind her.

"Going to get wet around here before the day's over," Julia commented, looking up from the table. Uncharacteristically, she was clad only in an old terrycloth robe and a floppy pair of slippers, her uncombed hair hanging loosely around her face.

Without makeup, Susannah thought, *Julia looks every one of her forty years.*

"Be a good day to curl up in front of the fireplace with a good book," Julia added.

"I wish I could." Pouring a mug of coffee, Susannah sat down across the table from her stepmother. "But I've got to go down to San Diego this morning."

"San Diego?" Julia glanced up, brushing a strand of hair back from her eyes. "What on earth for?"

"To pick up my car, for one thing." Susannah hesitated a moment, then plunged ahead. "I've decided to keep the company, Julia. I don't think Dad would have left it to me if he'd wanted me to just sell out or to hire a manager and function as an absentee owner."

"You're going to run it yourself?" Julia raised an eyebrow, then asked cautiously, "Don't you think that might be a little too much for you?"

"I'm getting a little tired of everyone telling me what a dumb mistake it would be for me to run the company!" Susannah gulped at her coffee, cursing as the hot liquid scorched her mouth. Glaring, she dabbed at her lips with a napkin. "I wouldn't have expected it from you."

"Hey, just a minute. I didn't say it would be a mistake. I just asked if maybe it wouldn't be too big a job for you to take on, that's all. Go for it!" As Julia grinned, the years fell away, and she suddenly looked much younger. "Show those chauvinistic bastards what a real woman can do."

"Yeah." Somewhat mollified, Susannah gingerly sipped at her coffee. It had cooled a little and went down easily. "Well, I'm sure it won't be easy," she admitted. "I've had the education, but my practical experience is very limited." Her lips twisted as she took another sip of coffee. "My boss is of the old school—a woman's place is in the kitchen, preferably barefoot and pregnant. What I've done for the past few years is shuffle papers, for the most part. I think I can do it, though. Dad taught me a lot about the business when I was growing up. I was setting forms, tying wire, and running bulldozers before I was out of junior high school."

"How I remember!" Julia smiled wryly. "I almost had a heart attack when Josh let you run that D-9 Cat up at Lake Arrowhead. I'm sure that knowing a little about the building trades is a plus, but will it be enough? You're going to be dealing with one of the most macho class of men left in the country, you know, and they might not take too kindly to being bossed by a twenty-six-year-old female." Julia picked up the half-empty cigarette pack in front of her, then pushed it away with an expression of disgust. "Some of the stories Josh told me—"

"The old days of brute force are gone," Susannah interrupted firmly. "A foreman or superintendent is no longer picked for his job because he can whip any man on his crew. They're chosen for their brains these days, and whether or not they can bring a job in on schedule and within budget. Besides, I won't be out in the field pushing a crew. I'll be in the office."

"Well, I wish you luck," Julia said. "You're going to need it. And if there's ever anything I can do, just holler."

"Thanks. I might just take you up on that." Susannah sipped her coffee for a moment, smiling as she tried to imagine what Adam McBride's reaction to her decision would be. He'd made it crystal clear what he thought of women in a man's world. With a slight shake of her head she looked back at Julia. "What are your plans for today?"

Julia sighed. "As soon as I can drag these old bones into the shower, I've got to get dressed and go to the bank to make sure there's enough cash in checking to run this place for a while." She paused, picking up her cup and draining it, then patting her lips dry with a napkin. "Then, after the bank, I've got a meeting with Charles Thomas, Josh's insurance agent. All in all, it's going to be a busy day. Why do you ask?"

"Would you mind giving me a ride to the airport when you're ready to leave?"

"Sure, no problem."

An hour later, Julia pulled to a stop at the curb in front of the terminal building at Ontario Airport. Susannah walked into the busy terminal and gasped in dismay at the long lines in front of the ticket counters.

Sighing, she hitched the strap of her shoulder bag up a little higher, then elbowed her way through the crowd toward the Pacific Southwest Airlines counter, where she was relieved to discover a seat available on a flight leaving in less than an hour.

After passing through the security check, she found an empty seat in the passenger lounge. The vast room was crowded for the first few minutes, then a departure on one of the other airlines was announced and most of the people in the room stood and began moving toward the loading ramps. Susannah leaned back in her chair, gratefully stretching her legs in the newly vacated space, and glanced at the large clock on the wall. Forty-five minutes to wait. Since she had brought nothing to read, she amused herself by studying the other passengers and those people waiting to greet incoming flights.

A few rows away from her seat, a neatly dressed young man sat leafing through a magazine, glancing every few seconds at the small girl who was sitting quietly by his side. *Like Adam and his daughter,* she thought, wondering if the little girl missed her mother as much as Adam's daughter probably missed hers. After a few minutes, the child pointed excitedly toward a group of arriving passengers and tugged at her father's sleeve. "Mommy!" she shrieked, spoiling Susannah's illusion. Susannah watched the young family's reunion, smiling enviously at the happy, excited manner in which they all embraced. *Obviously,* she thought, *they're very much in love.* She felt strangely disappointed when they left the waiting room, chattering happily.

Watching the endless variety of people moving through the room, time passed quickly, and before long she was aboard a 737 streaking southward, the airliner bursting through the heavy cloud cover into the sunlight like a fish jumping from a murky pond.

The sky over San Diego was bright and sunny, scented by a cool, salty breeze from the ocean. She hailed a taxi in front of the terminal, and half an hour later she was unlocking the front door of her apartment.

As always, when returning from a prolonged absence, it was relaxing to return to her own place, to be alone among her own things, with no need to make polite conversation to anyone. She moved contentedly around the apartment, watering her plants and sorting through the pile of mail that had accumulated beneath the slot in the front door. Personal letters and bills she put aside to look at later; everything else she tossed into a wastebasket without a second glance.

After washing up and changing into a fresh blouse to

go with her blue suit, she left the apartment, heading downstairs to the garage beneath the apartments. She gazed at the small, low-slung, candy apple–red roadster for a few moments before unlocking the door, remembering the day it had been purchased.

She'd been wavering for some time between a Datsun 280Z and a Corvette, enduring her father's good-natured teasing about not being able to make up her mind. The car would be her first major purchase after graduation and accepting the position with the U.S. Navy; and the idea of committing herself to such big monthly payments had been terrifying.

"Hell, girl," Josh had chuckled, "wait until you're dealing for a new D-9 Cat! That'll make this thing seem like a dime-store purchase."

In the end she'd selected the Corvette, and the day she'd driven it from the dealership to her father's house in Upland, he'd met her in the driveway, a thick shop manual for the car in his hand.

"If you're going to drive it, you're going to understand it," he declared, thrusting the manual into her hands. Pulling the shiny new car into the garage, he'd jacked up the front end, then pulled a mechanic's creeper from a peg on the wall and handed it to her. "Crawl under," he directed.

When she was on her back, just before she rolled herself under the car, he handed her the manual. "Trace your suspension system today, honey. Go through that whole section in the book and compare it with the real thing. Check it all out. Find the grease fittings and oil drain plugs."

"I bought it to drive," she'd grumbled, "not to overhaul."

"Get under there," he said gruffly. "No daughter of mine is ever going to be standing alongside some freeway in the middle of the night, completely helpless because she's got a flat tire and doesn't know how to change it. That sheepskin of yours says you're an engineer—act like one . . ."

Now, as she climbed in under the wheel and switched on the ignition, she felt a surge of gratitude toward her father. Thanks to the knowledge he had bullied her into acquiring, the Corvette ran as smoothly now as it had when it was new, over four years ago. She changed the oil and filters frequently and performed all the routine minor maintenance as well. A year ago, when the front disc brake pads had worn out, she had installed new ones herself, Josh looking on with paternal pride.

She drove carefully through the residential neighborhood until she came to the on ramp of the freeway, where she accelerated smoothly into the traffic, heading south toward the Coronado Bridge exit. Fifteen minutes later, she was pulling into her own parking slot behind the huge, barnlike building that housed the Public Works Division on the North Island Naval Air Station.

She walked through the wide doors into the building, crossing the parking bay toward the row of offices housed on the opposite side of the building from the carpentry, welding, electric, and plumbing shops, her low heels clicking smartly on the smooth concrete floor.

"Susannah, what are you doing here today?" Gladys Worthing, the clerk-typist who served as secretary for Susannah and her boss, the facilities management officer, looked up from her crossword puzzle in surprise. "You're supposed to be on vacation."

"Vacation's over, Gladys." Susannah stopped in front of Gladys's desk and leaned forward confidentially. "Is his lordship in?" she asked, jerking her thumb toward the door of her supervisor's office.

"You're in luck," Gladys replied dryly. "He's honoring us with his presence today. He called in this morning, but I told him he had that meeting with the commander, so he came on in."

"Good. I need to see him." Susannah hesitated a moment, then stuck out her hand. "It's been nice working with you, Gladys—even if I can't say the same for his nibs."

"You—you're *quitting?*"

"That's right," Susannah answered cheerfully.

"You're going to walk out on a good, secure civil service job"—Gladys stared, appalled—"just like *that?*"

Susannah snapped her fingers. "Just like that," she confirmed. "Type up a resignation form for me, will you?"

As she turned toward the door of John Dowling's office, she saw Gladys snatch up the phone. Susannah smiled wryly at Gladys's haste to share this latest tidbit with her friends in the supply branch.

"Oh, hello, love." Dowling peered up over the rim of his glasses as Susannah opened the door and peeked in. "Come in, come in. Keep me company. It's lonely at the top."

Hiding a smile, Susannah took a seat in the chair to the right of Dowling's large, polished desk. *Only GS-13's and above rate such desks,* she thought, but she would have been willing to bet a month's pay that no other GS-13 on the installation could boast of such a pristinely bare desk, gleaming with polish. A retired army colonel with old-fashioned, aristocratic bearing, John Dowling peered down his rather prominent bony nose at the rest of the world from a height of six feet two. The glossy, barren desktop was an accurate reflection of his cavalier attitude toward paperwork: "Take it away, love," he would murmur, when Susannah or Gladys troubled him with day-to-day paperwork that required his signature. "You take care of it. I'll sign it later . . . Listen, love, did I ever tell you about the time I was wounded in the Battle of the Bulge?"

"How are you, John?" Susannah asked now, crossing her legs and settling herself comfortably in the chair.

"Well, that depends, love." Dowling linked hands behind his silvery head and leaned back in the padded swivel chair, regarding her with an amiable leer. "I'm not as good as I once was, but I'm as good *once* as I ever was . . ." His voice trailed off, a look of irritation crossing his face.

"Which reminds me—where the hell have you been

the last few days? I thought you were supposed to handle the old man today, but Gladys called me—"

"John, I've been on my annual leave," Susannah reminded him.

"Leave? Why in hell doesn't anyone around here keep me informed of these things?"

"You signed my leave papers, John. It's entered on the schedule as well, if you'd ever bother to look at it." She was unable to hide her amusement at the expression of consternation that appeared on his face, only to be quickly wiped away.

"Well, if you're on leave," he muttered after a moment, "what're you doing here?"

"I came to resign. I've got almost two weeks of leave left, so that can serve as my notice."

"Resign?" he exclaimed, the expression of consternation returning at once. He sat forward, frowning at her as if she'd dropped something small, wet, and nasty on his desktop. "Why, you can't resign *now*, for Christ's sake. What about the annual inspections next month? I'll never be able to get another engineer hired and in here by then."

"My father died a few days ago, John," she began quietly. "He left his construction company to me, and I've decided to run it for a while." She paused for a moment, thinking. "If you absolutely insist, I'll work another week after my vacation is over, but that's all. And," she added quickly, as a cunning expression began forming on the old man's face, "that is final."

Dowling scowled angrily toward the window of his office for a moment, twisting a pencil in his fingers. Abruptly he snapped it in two, tossing the pieces on the floor.

"No, to hell with it. If you're quitting, go ahead and do it. But you'll never get another job like *this*, Susannah."

Slowly she got to her feet, trembling with anger in spite of the fact that he had reacted exactly as she had anticipated. It was so typical of him that he'd not offered one word of sympathy for the loss of her father, concerning himself only with the nuisance her quitting was going to cause for him.

"I sincerely hope so," she said distinctly.

As she reached the door of his office, Dowling gave a scornful little laugh. "What kind of a nut are you, anyway?" he asked. "You really think you're enough of an engineer to run a construction company?"

She hesitated for a moment with her hand on the doorknob, fighting the almost overwhelming urge to retort. With an effort she calmed herself. As she pulled the door shut behind herself, she relegated John Dowling to the past with an almost giddy sensation of relief. For the first time she realized that her life had been way past due for a change; her father's death had provided the impetus, but she knew she would have had to leave her job soon even if he had lived. Shuffling bureaucratic paperwork and escorting visiting naval officers around the facility while her boss relived the glory of his war was not the reason she had obtained an engineering degree.

She stopped at Gladys's desk and signed her resignation papers, then crossed the parking bays into the shops, where she said good-bye to the men she'd come to like and respect during her years of employment—the building tradesmen who went out with their trucks and tools and actually worked at their crafts. It had been these men who had made the past four years bearable, and it was with genuine regret that she bid them good-bye.

Clouds were forming on the horizon as she drove away from the station, crossing the Coronado Bridge back to the mainland. When she left her apartment for the second time that afternoon, fat raindrops were beginning to pelt against the windshield of the Corvette, and she drove carefully on the rain-slick streets, encapsulated in the small cockpit with a Jimmy Dorsey cassette in the stereo tape deck, the sweet music erasing the unpleasant memory of her encounter with John Dowling. Because of the weather, it was after nine o'clock in the evening when she arrived in Upland, where she went to bed and fell into a deep, dreamless sleep.

After a light, hasty breakfast the following morning she dressed in faded, comfortable blue jeans and an old loose sweater, then drove down to the industrial park where the Lockwood and Sons yard was located. The company occupied ten acres between a cabinet manufacturing plant and a building supplier's warehouse, less than ten minutes' drive from her father's—*Julia's, now*, she corrected herself.

The lot was surrounded by a tall, chain-link fence, with a wide gate at the street entrance, which was kept locked during nonworking hours. Against the fence at the back of the lot, the huge, tin maintenance shed loomed, silhouetted against the mountains. Off to each side of the maintenance shed, storage buildings and equipment sheds butted up against the fence. To the right as she drove through the gate, a stucco building that had at one time been a three-bedroom house now served as headquarters for most of the office staff. Several cars, she observed with satisfaction, were parked behind the office, indicating that most of the staff was at work.

She turned left inside the gate, stopping in front of the old double-wide mobile home that Josh had used as an office for as long as she could remember. As she got out of the Corvette, she looked around the huge yard, frowning at the sight of two D-9 Caterpillar tractors parked near the rear fence, their huge dozer blades and steel treads coated with a dull, brick-red layer of rust. A large skip loader was parked in front of the maintenance shed, the front end jacked up and the two front wheels removed. From within the shed the flickering light from an arc welder and the rattling whir of an air wrench told her that the mechanics were hard at work.

She stood for a moment on the wooden step of the mobile home, looking around at the rest of the yard. Stacks of old tires and wheels, sections of conveyor belt, and other large metal parts were stacked in various locations, giving the appearance, to the uninitiated, of a rather neatly kept junkyard. Susannah knew better: the assorted "junk" in the yard represented several thousand dollars worth of machinery parts. She opened the door and stepped into the office.

"Why, hello, Susannah!" Fran Parker, her father's longtime secretary, looked up from her desk and beamed. "It's good to see you again. I didn't have a chance to talk to you at Mr. Morgan's office the other day, but . . ."

"How've you been, Fran?" Susannah asked. "Keeping busy?"

"Oh, there's always something to do," Fran assured her. "I manage to stay busy. Susie, I'm so sorry about Josh, I—"

"Yes, me, too, Fran. Thanks." Susannah turned and looked out through the front window. "Listen, Fran, get the office types over here, will you? And if any of the superintendents or foremen are here, have them come as well. Oh—and be sure to have Bill Fredrickson come, if he's in the shop."

With a startled glance Fran reached for the phone. Susannah walked on down the hallway and entered her father's office.

She sat in the swivel chair behind the battered desk, looking around the small, familiar room with an almost unbearable sensation of nostalgia, remembering many happy hours here with her father. The walls were covered with photographs and memorabilia from various jobs, along with the inevitable "girlie" calendars provided by tool salesmen and company representatives eager to do business with the company. There was also a calendar on the wall that featured a large, full-color illustration of an open-pit mine, impossibly long conveyors carrying raw ore up to the surface. A metal filing cabinet stood against the opposite wall, a stack of cardboard boxes leaning against it.

She leaned back in the chair for a moment and closed

her eyes, her father's presence seeming very real in the aromas of cherry pipe tobacco, sweat, leather, and oil that permeated the small room. At the sound of heavy footsteps approaching the office, she opened her eyes and sat up alertly.

"Morning, Susannah." Glen Vincent entered the room, nodding coolly. "So it's true, eh?"

"What's true, Glen?"

"That you're going to try running the company." Vincent shook his head dolefully. "Bad mistake, if you ask me."

"Nobody asked you," she replied, swallowing the anger that rose up in her throat at his words. She nodded a greeting as Fred Ward entered the room and sank gratefully onto one of the folding metal chairs. "Fred, how are you?" she asked.

"Fine, thanks." Fred, a sixtyish, heavyset man with a full head of wavy white hair, was the chief planner and estimator for the company and had been with her father from the beginning. Fred glanced up at Vincent, an inquiring expression on his ruddy, fleshy face. "What's all this about, Glen?"

"How should I know?" Vincent grunted. "Ask her—she's the boss."

"That right?" Fred peered at Susannah for a moment through narrowed eyes, then shook his head and looked away.

Three more men entered the room together, their footsteps causing the old mobile home to shake. Bill Fredrickson, the master mechanic, followed by Ralph Whitman and Adam McBride, all entered the office and squeezed up against the walls, looking at one another with quizzical expressions. Susannah's heart skipped a beat when Adam looked at her and raised an eyebrow, then nodded knowingly, as if he alone knew the reason for the summons.

"Good morning, fellows," Susannah said, including them all in the greeting. "Adam, would you shut the door, please?"

When the door was secure, Susannah took a deep breath and began. "I know you've all been wondering what's going to become of the company, what's going to happen to your jobs, and so on. I can set your minds at ease about that: each man in this room is secure in his position, and as long as he continues to cut the mustard, his job is safe. Now—"

"Hold on a second," Bill Fredrickson interrupted, a surprised expression on his blunt-featured face. "Are you sayin' that you—Susannah, are *you* gonna run things from here on out?"

She looked at the stocky, muscular man in the greasy overalls for a moment. Bill Fredrickson enjoyed a well-deserved reputation as one of the finest heavy-duty diesel mechanics in the state, and retaining his services was vital to the continued success of the company. If she lost him . . .

"Yes, Bill," she said evenly, "that's exactly what it means. Is that a problem for you?"

Before Bill had a chance to reply, Glen Vincent gave a snort of laughter, shaking his head. "Hell, I've tried to talk to her, Bill, but she won't listen to my warnings. She—"

"You warned me, all right," Susannah cut him off sharply. "Now, let me warn you: you're either part of the solution around here, or you're part of the problem. If you're unhappy about continuing around here, I'm sure there must be dozens of companies who would be happy to grab a man of your experience. What's it going to be, Glen?"

"All right, Susannah," Vincent muttered after the tension in the crowded office had grown for several moments. "I'm on your team, I guess." He looked down, his face flaming with humiliation, and Susannah realized that no matter what he'd said, he would never forgive her.

"I'm glad to hear that, Glen," she said quietly. She looked over at Fredrickson, who had been following the exchange closely, as had the other men. "Bill?"

Fredrickson suddenly grinned, his teeth startlingly white against his swarthy features. "I've been drawin' my paychecks here for ten years," he drawled. "None of 'em have bounced yet. Long's they don't start now, I'm with you."

Susannah relaxed, feeling the tension drain out of the small room. The other men shifted into more comfortable positions, waiting expectantly for her to continue. Adam was staring at her with an expression of reluctant admiration, and he winked slightly as their eyes met.

"Good. We all know where we stand. Now, I'd like a report from each of you on the status of your departments. Glen, would you like to start it off?"

"Well, the money situation isn't too bad," Vincent began, his voice trembling slightly. He drew a breath before continuing. "The housing pad job over in Etiwanda is right on schedule, and the money has been coming in quarterly, as agreed in the contract. First State Bank's financing the job, as usual . . .

"We've got a crew moving dirt on the new industrial park in east Ontario, and various other small jobs are going on around the area, so most of our crews are busy." He paused for a moment, seeming to become more confident.

"Now, on the debit side, we've got a payment coming up to Thompson Tractor on the purchase rental of the new D-9. County property taxes are coming up soon—I'm working on them—and of course we have our weekly payroll to meet. All in all, we *are* operating in the black at the present time—but just barely."

Susannah thought she detected a gleam of malice in his eyes as he said this, but she couldn't be sure. "Any new jobs scheduled for the near future?"

"Yeah, enough to keep plugging along, paying the bills," Fred Ward said in his deep, gravelly voice. "Nothing really big, though. An industrial building going up in Cucamonga, a piece of that pipeline coming over from San Berdo, scheduled to start in March." Frowning, he shifted in the chair, which groaned beneath his bulk.

"Josh and I worked up a good bid on that San Gabriel Canyon job, but we haven't heard from them yet. That's the one we need, Susannah. We get that job, we'll be up there with the big boys. That job'll make us or break us, if we get it."

Susannah nodded thoughtfully. "We can't count on 'ifs,' Fred. We'd better get somebody out to sell some work . . . Bill, I noticed a couple of dozers parked out by the fence. Is there a maintenance problem?"

"Naw, they're ready to go. We're puttin' new brakes on the 966 skip loader today, and I've got a couple of the boys welding reinforcement on dozer blades and loader buckets out back. But I'm beginnin' to have to scratch for work to keep my crew busy, and I don't like that."

Susannah nodded again. "Adam? Ralph? Any comments?"

Adam cleared his throat as if to speak, then shook his head and remained silent. Ralph just turned toward the door, muttering something about getting back to his crew.

"Okay, that's it then," Susannah said, getting to her feet as the men began to file out of the office. Vincent was hanging back, she noticed, as if he had something further to say. "I want to thank you all for staying with me, and I look forward to working with you."

"Same here," Fredrickson put in, grinning at Vincent before turning to leave. A moment later they trooped down the wooden steps of the trailer, returning to their various duties, and Susannah looked inquiringly at Vincent.

"Was there something else, Glen?" she asked.

"Just that I'd like you to reconsider, Susannah." Vincent watched her carefully as he spoke. "Especially now that you've been filled in on our actual position. I was kind of hoping you might have second thoughts about selling out. I can guarantee a fair price, and if you're worried about the men, I think I can safely promise that they'd all keep their jobs with the new owners." He paused, an expression of desperation crossing his face, a look almost of fear, Susannah thought. "This is the final offer. Take it, for God's sake!"

"No," she declared bluntly. "If that's not clear enough, Glen, I'll have Fran type it up for my signature."

"That won't be necessary," he replied in a strangled-sounding voice. With clinical detachment Susannah noticed that his face was a dark red. "I hope none of us will regret your decision."

"Indeed," Susannah agreed, gesturing toward the open door of the office. "Now, I have a lot to do."

She stood in the doorway until she heard Vincent close the outer door and troop down the steps, then she sighed and called, "Fran, would you come here, please?"

"I couldn't help overhearing," Fran said excitedly when she appeared in the doorway. "I just want to say congratulations! What can I do for you, boss?"

Susannah grinned at the older woman. "For one thing, call me Susannah, like always. For another, would you mind going over to the main building and picking up a copy of the bid Dad worked up on the San Gabriel Canyon job? I'd like to look it over."

"Sure thing." With another delighted smile Fran hurried away. In a few seconds Susannah heard the outer office door close behind her.

Sighing heavily, she sank down in the swivel chair behind her father's desk, trying to shake off the jitters that had descended on her slim shoulders like a cold, wet blanket. She had an inescapable suspicion that she had plunged into icy waters that were well over her head. The initial crisis—breaking the news to her key personnel—was over, but now, she realized, all these experienced construction veterans were relying on her to keep the company alive and profitable. For a moment the panic threatened to destroy her resolve, then she remembered John Dowling's scornful laugh, and the fear was driven away by anger and renewed determination. She would show him. She would show them all.

Sitting up straighter in the chair, she reached for the pile of mail that had accumulated on one corner of her father's desk and began sorting through it, tossing most of it into the wastebasket. When she felt the trailer shift beneath the weight of someone entering from outside, she assumed it was Fran returning with the papers she'd been asked for and didn't look up until she heard a tap on the doorjamb of her office. She glanced up in surprise. A beefy, middle-aged man dressed in a gray business suit stood in the open doorway, a thick manila envelope clutched in his hand.

"Hi, cutie," he said, looking her over with lewd speculation in his pale-blue eyes. "Run and get the boss, will you? I've got some news he's gonna be glad to hear."

CHAPTER FOUR

"Thanks for coming by in person, Mr. Harkness. I can't understand why somebody hasn't gotten back to you on this by now, but I'll look into it." Getting to her feet, Susannah forced herself to smile, masking the deep anger at what she had just learned. "I'll let you know as soon as we set a starting date for the job."

"Fine, that's just fine. The sooner the better, though. We'd like to have a lot of that material moved out before the next rainy season sets in." Harkness shrugged, looking a little embarrassed. "Look, uh, I'm sorry about the way I came in here today. I just wasn't expecting to see a —a young woman in the boss's office. I just assumed—"

"It's quite all right, Mr. Harkness. A week ago, I didn't expect to be sitting here either." She walked with him toward the front door of the trailer, noticing that Fran was still away from her desk. The secretary had been gone for more than half an hour, plenty of time to have found the papers she'd been sent for. *On the other hand,* Susannah thought grimly, *perhaps she's not getting the cooperation she needs in locating the papers.*

"I suppose we'll be seeing plenty of each other in the next several months." Smiling, Harkness offered his hand, and Susannah shook it firmly. "Congratulations . . . and good luck."

"Thanks." She stood in the open doorway of the trailer, watching until Harkness's gleaming new Buick rolled out the gate and receded in the distance. Back in her office she picked up the manila envelope Harkness had just delivered, then marched across the graveled

51

yard toward the office building, her eyes snapping with anger.

Fran looked up, an apologetic expression on her face, as Susannah burst in through the door. Fran was kneeling in front of a large filing cabinet, papers and folders scattered on the floor all around her.

"Susannah, I just don't understand it," she began. "I know darned well those papers were in this drawer, but I can't find them."

Standing just inside the door, Susannah looked around the large room. Fred Ward sat at his desk on one side of the room, a telephone propped on one shoulder, talking in low tones into the mouthpiece. At the rear of the room, silhouetted against a window, Glen Vincent sat tapping the keyboard of a computer terminal, frequently glancing at a sheaf of bills and invoices spread across his desk.

"Never mind, Fran," Susannah said. "Just go on back to the office. Thanks for trying."

"But I—" As Fran looked again at the expression on Susannah's face, she cut her protest short and quickly left the room.

Fred Ward concluded his telephone conversation, then glanced around and nodded at Susannah. She ignored him, glaring at Glen Vincent, seemingly oblivious to anyone else in the room.

"Uh-oh," Fred muttered softly. He picked up his coffee cup and sidled out of the room, going toward the back of the house where the coffeepot was located.

Vincent finally looked up. When he saw the expression on her face, he sighed audibly, then reached out and switched the computer off. There was a kind of finality in the gesture that was deeply satisfying to Susannah.

"Okay, so now you know." Vincent spoke in a resigned tone of voice. "Am I fired, or do I get the chance to resign?"

"Just so you're out of here today." Susannah's voice was taut with anger. She stepped toward him, brandishing the manila envelope. "You *knew*. All along, you *knew* we were the successful bidders on the San Gabriel Canyon job! How long did you think you could keep it secret, Glen?"

"Just long enough to talk you into selling the company." Wearily Vincent shook out a cigarette and lit it, a bitterly resigned expression on his face. "Hell, I knew this morning I'd had it when you turned my offer down so flatly. I'd hoped to just sort of slip away and avoid all this, but I suppose you feel entitled to your pound of flesh."

"Does anybody else know about this?" she asked, indicating the envelope.

"Nope, just me. Me and some, ah, potential investors, none of whom are Lockwood employees." He smiled crookedly as he took a drag of his cigarette. "I'm the only traitor, Susannah."

"I see." She sat down at Fred Ward's desk, cradling the thick manila envelope on her lap. After a moment she heard the sound of Vincent cleaning his personal things from his desk.

"You know, Fred was right," Vincent said conversationally. "That canyon job'll make you or break you. And as close to the bone as Josh bid it, it'll probably break you."

"Well, that's no longer your concern." Susannah got to her feet and stared expressionlessly. "Just clear out today, Vincent. And don't make the mistake of asking Lockwood and Sons for a reference."

"You're getting off to a hell of a start, aren't you?" He chuckled wryly. "First day on the job you fire the second oldest employee in the company. Yep, your old man would be proud of you, Susannah."

"Leave my father out of this." She stared at him with distaste. "I'm just glad he never had to find out what a treacherous bastard you really are, Vincent." Without taking her eyes off him, she raised her voice. "Fred! Would you mind stepping in here, please?"

Fred returned to the room, carrying a cup of coffee.

The expression on his face indicated he'd heard enough of the conversation to know what was going on.

"Vincent won't be working for us any longer, Fred," Susannah stated flatly. "Please see that he takes only his personal belongings with him when he leaves, will you?"

Fred nodded, looking uncomfortable.

Susannah left the room without looking at Vincent again. As she walked back toward the trailer, she couldn't help thinking about the man's parting shot. *It is a hell of a start,* she admitted to herself, *but what choice did I have?* With all the unpleasantness in her life lately, it was time for something nice to happen, way past time.

"Fran, who at the bank handles the Lockwood account?" she asked as she stepped into the trailer.

"Greg McGruder." She looked up curiously as Susannah stopped at her desk. "What was all that about?" she asked, pointing in the direction of the office building.

"Glen Vincent was trying to sabotage the company so he and his partners could buy it cheap," Susannah replied, realizing that the truth would be preferable to misinformed speculation. "The day after Dad died, the company was notified that we were the successful bidders on the canyon job. Vincent was here alone that day, so he took the call and kept quiet about it, hoping I'd be eager to get rid of the company, and he and his partners could pick it up for a song."

"I never have liked that man." Fran pressed her lips together as she shook her head. "Never. I've worked here for fifteen years, and he's rarely had a pleasant word for me. I'm glad he's gone."

"Fran, would you call McGruder and set up an appointment for me as soon as possible? We need to arrange financing for the canyon job." She started to leave, then stopped. "While you're at it, we're going to need a replacement for Vincent. Put an ad in the paper, will you?"

As she walked toward her office, Fran was picking up the phone. Susannah spent the remainder of the morning studying the bid her father and Fred Ward had submitted on the canyon job, poring over the maps and drawings with a growing feeling of unease. When she finally pushed the papers away, she admitted to herself that Vincent had been correct: Josh's bid *had* been very "close to the bone." She took a battery-powered calculator from the top drawer of the desk and began punching in figures, feeling her spirits sink as the totals mounted relentlessly. It was going to require skillful planning for the job to be accomplished in a way that would allow the company to earn even a nominal profit.

"Susannah?" Fran tapped on her door, interrupting her gloomy thoughts. "I was able to get you an appointment for this afternoon, right after lunch." She glanced at her watch. "Speaking of which, how about joining me? I was just getting ready to go out for a bite."

"As long as it's no place fancy, I guess." She looked at the immaculate beige pantsuit Fran was wearing and smiled ruefully. "I'm not exactly dressed for a nice place," she admitted, indicating her faded jeans and loose sweater with a gesture.

"Well, I was thinking of a hamburger." Fran smiled. "How's that sound to you?"

"Sounds just fine, Fran."

"Good. Let's take my car," Fran suggested. "I'm afraid of those little sports cars like yours."

Following a quick lunch, during which Fran told her new boss something of the quirks and foibles of the office staff with whom she would be working in the future, Susannah returned to the yard to pick up her own car. She drove home, where she changed into a skirt, sweater, and matching jacket and a pair of heels for her meeting at the bank. She ran a brush through her short, wavy hair, peering critically into the mirror, and decided against applying makeup. Five minutes later she was driving toward the bank, her heart filled with optimism.

It was with vastly different spirits that she returned to the office just two hours later. She marched into the trailer, her face a grim mask, ignoring Fran's bright greeting.

"Can you round up Adam McBride and Fred Ward for me?"

"Troubles?" Fran asked as she reached for the phone.

"Troubles."

Back in her office she sat down with a pad of paper and a pen, pulling the calculator over and flicking it on. Half an hour later, she was no closer to a solution than she had been when she left the bank. She pushed the calculator away with an exasperated sigh.

Josh *must* have had something in mind; he would never have placed the company in this position out of ignorance. He must have had a plan—but whatever it was, it had apparently died with him that night in the San Gabriel Canyon . . .

"You wanted to see me, boss?" Adam appeared in the doorway, a slightly mocking smile on his face. After looking at her for a moment, he abruptly sobered. "Hey, it can't be as bad as all that, Susie," he said, a note of concern in his voice.

"I'm afraid it's about as bad as it can get, Adam." She smiled wearily, wondering at the way her spirits lifted at the sight of him, despite the troubling events of the day so far. "Have a seat, Adam. Fred should be here in a minute. I need the benefit of your experience."

"You're welcome to that anytime." He sat down, hitching his chair closer to her desk. He reached out and patted her hand, giving it a little squeeze before releasing it. She experienced a pleasant tingle at the contact, and in spite of her worry, she found herself returning his warm smile. "Listen, no matter what's going on, you still have to eat. How about having dinner with me tonight?"

Her eyes flooded at his kind words, and she quickly ducked her head, nodding. "That sounds great, Adam. Maybe it'll cheer me up."

"Just part of the service, lady." He leaned back in his chair. "I'll go home and clean up as soon as we finish here, then I'll take you to this really terrific place I know—"

"No margaritas, though, okay?" she interrupted with a shaky little laugh. She was feeling better by the moment. Adam's presence, she realized with a vague sense of astonishment, was like a tonic to her.

"No margaritas," he agreed, smiling. He turned as Fred Ward entered the small office. "Hi, Fred. Here we are again, it seems. Where's Vincent? Shouldn't he be in on this?"

"You mean you haven't heard?" Fred nodded toward Susannah with an ironic grin. "The boss tied a can to his tail this morning."

"You're kidding!" Adam gaped at Susannah, and she quickly filled him in on the reason why Vincent had been fired.

"The sonofabitch!" Adam exclaimed when she was finished. "I knew he had a crooked streak in him, but I never would have figured him for anything that blatant." He shook his head, then looked over at Susannah. "I guess your father's will just about did him in."

"Yeah, he was figuring to inherit a nice piece of the company," Fred Ward rumbled in his deep voice. "Looks like he figured if he couldn't get it honestly, he'd try and steal it."

"I'm sorry it had to happen, but that's not what I called you two guys in here to talk about." Susannah glanced at the figures spread across her desk and sighed heavily before continuing. "The bank won't finance the canyon project."

"They *won't?*" Fred exclaimed. "But—but they've been financing our jobs for the last fifteen years!"

"Yeah, for Dad," Susannah said glumly. "It seems that, in their opinion, I don't have enough business experience to justify the financing, especially the way the job is currently written."

"The way it's currently written?" Fred asked, leaning

forward in his chair, frowning. "What's that supposed to mean?"

"I was afraid of this," Adam put in. "I've been over those figures, Fred. The way it looked to me, there just wasn't enough overhead built into this estimate."

"That's what Mr. McGruder said," Susannah said flatly. "Not enough margin for emergencies, breakdowns . . . he suggested we take on a partner and make it a joint venture."

"That's no damned good," Fred Ward shot back quickly. "Lockwood and Sons have never gone in for joint ventures. For one thing you always seem to wind up squabbling over the money. It's hard to agree on who has overall control."

"Besides, the only outfit around here that might have the resources for a job like that is Groat—and we sure don't want to get involved with those turkeys," Adam stated grimly.

"No, that's for sure." Fred shook his head slowly. "They have a mighty bad reputation. In fact, I doubt if Harkness's people would agree to Groat Construction even if we wanted them in on the job." Sighing, he lit a cigarette, narrowing his eyes as he exhaled a cloud of smoke. "You know, I had the feeling when Josh and I were writing the bid that he had something up his sleeve, but when I asked him about it, he just grinned and shook his head. Said he didn't want to spoil the surprise in case we got the job." He sighed again, staring at the glowing tip of his cigarette. "Well, here we are with the job, and I still don't have any idea what the hell he had in mind."

"Yeah, he really left us holding the bag." Adam glanced apologetically at Susannah, then paused and asked, "Well, what are you going to do?"

The question stunned her at first, then she realized that this was what being the owner and chief operating officer of a construction company meant. Subconsciously she realized that she'd been hoping Adam or Fred would have some kind of solution. As she looked at their expectant faces, the reality of her position settled upon her like a heavy weight.

"At this moment," she confessed, "I don't have the faintest idea. Maybe something will come to me soon."

"Christ, I hope so," Fred added sourly, his expression clearly indicating his opinion of that possibility. He got to his feet, leaning over with a grunt to stab out his cigarette in the ashtray on the desk. "I'll be thinking about it, too, but don't pin your hopes on me, folks. Now, unless there's something else, it's quitting time for me."

"Good night, Fred," Susannah said. "Thanks for all the help today."

"Oh, hell, I didn't do anything." He paused, a sudden grin transforming his ruddy, fleshy face, giving it the momentary illusion of youthful handsomeness. "Except maybe for making sure Vince didn't haul off half the office when he left." He paused, sobering abruptly. "Damn, that reminds me—I forgot to ask him for his keys to the office and yard."

"I'll give him a call and ask him to mail them in or drop them off." Fred nodded, looking slightly guilty as he turned and left the room. Susannah smiled at Adam as the front door opened and closed. "He's a good man, isn't he?"

"Worth his weight in gold around here." Adam paused, frowning. "Which makes that bid all the harder to understand, Susie. All I can figure is that Josh bid real low in order to clinch getting the job"—he shrugged bewilderedly—"which doesn't do us much good now, of course. But if we just knew what he'd had in mind . . ."

Fran appeared in the doorway. "Susannah, do you need me for anything else?"

"No, go ahead, Fran. I'll see you tomorrow." She leaned back in her chair, stretching, then got to her feet. "I'm ready to go home myself."

"Good night, then."

When Fran was gone, Adam turned and smiled at Susannah. "See you in about an hour?" he asked softly.

She hesitated. "Will I be okay dressed like this?" she

asked, indicating the skirt and jacket she'd worn for her meeting at the bank. "Or should I change?"

"You look just fine the way you are," he answered, his eyes glowing with admiration.

"Then come for me just as soon as you're ready," she said, warmed by his words and the expression on his face.

Although it wasn't yet five o'clock as they left the trailer, it was almost completely dark, a fiery red streak painted low across the western horizon providing only a dim glow of illumination to the winter sky. Susannah climbed into her car and switched on the ignition. Ten minutes later she pulled into the driveway and parked next to Julia's Eldorado.

She found her stepmother in the kitchen, tossing an enormous green salad. Julia smiled when Susannah entered the family room and took a seat at the breakfast counter across from her.

"Well, how was your first day as a construction magnate?"

"Lousy, Julia, just lousy."

Susannah filled Julia in on the events of the day while Julia finished preparing her salad. The older woman listened closely, nodding and clucking in agreement or sympathy. When Susannah was finished, she patted her arm reassuringly.

"Everything will work out, you'll see," she assured her. "Now, let me tell you my news. I saw Josh's insurance agent today, and it seems there's some question about the double indemnity. You see, Charles Thomas has known Josh for years, and he knows that Josh hadn't taken a drink in over five years, ever since they discovered his diabetes. Charles *knows* Josh couldn't have been drunk."

"But what does that have to do with the double indemnity?" Susannah asked, then her face cleared. "Oh, I see."

"Exactly. If it *was* suicide, then the policy doesn't pay double indemnity. Charlie asked me if there was any reason to suspect that Josh might have wanted to take his own life." She looked away, biting her lip. "Naturally," she continued, her voice breaking a little, "I told him I had no reason to suspect any such thing." She looked up at Susannah then, her face crumbling as the tears began to flow down her cheeks. "But I tell you, honey, I just don't know *what* to think anymore!"

"Oh, Julia!" Susannah hurried around to the other side of the counter, taking the older woman in her arms, patting her back while Julia gradually regained control of herself. When Julia stepped back and reached for a napkin, Susannah asked, "What's going to happen with the insurance?"

Julia blew her nose before replying. "Charles is investigating. That's the word he used, Susannah—'investigating'—as if Josh were a criminal or something. When his investigation is complete, he'll make a recommendation to the company."

Deep in thought, Susannah resumed her seat at the counter. If it were true, if Josh *had* deliberately driven off that cliff to his death as Thomas suspected, there had to be a reason, a powerful one. Joshua Lockwood had been a man with such zest for life it was impossible for her to accept that he would have deliberately killed himself. Still, she had to admit that the suspicion had been gnawing at her—and unless she missed her guess, at Julia as well. Suddenly she experienced a surge of powerful anger at her father for doing what he had done to the two women who adored him so. The mess he had left his company in only compounded her resentment; the fact that he had doubtless had a plan for the San Gabriel Canyon job did her no good at all, none whatsoever.

The sudden chime of the doorbell was a welcome intrusion into her dark thoughts. Susannah hurried in to answer the door, looking forward to seeing Adam, to having him to herself for a few hours.

He stood in the doorway, smiling with those impossibly bright white teeth, looking so strong and confident that she experienced an almost overwhelming desire to throw herself into his arms. She smiled at him, drinking in reassurance and consolation from his smiling eyes.

"Come in, Adam."

Together they walked back to the family room. Susannah left him there with Julia while she went to get her coat. When she returned, Julia was staring appraisingly at Adam, taking in his freshly pressed brown slacks, tweed jacket, and glossy brown loafers with approval in her eyes.

"Don't mind me, Adam," she explained when he raised his eyebrows inquisitively. "I'm just not used to seeing you in anything but blue jeans and hard hats. You look very nice."

"Thanks, Julia. My baby-sitter charged me a dollar to press these slacks," he admitted with a rueful smile. "I haven't had them off the hanger in months." He turned to Susannah and pointed to the coat in her arms. "Better put that on. It's pretty chilly outside."

"You two have a nice time," Julia said.

"Julia, are you going to be all right?" As Susannah slipped into her coat, she suddenly felt guilty about leaving her stepmother alone, especially tonight. "Adam," she blurted, "would it be okay if Julia came with us? She's kind of blue tonight and probably shouldn't be alone."

"Nonsense," Julia declared. "I'm going to eat a steak and some salad, then curl up in front of the fireplace with a good book."

Susannah protested, but Julia remained adamant. "If you're really sure, then," Susannah said reluctantly.

"Go on, enjoy yourselves," Julia replied.

"I won't keep her too late," Adam put in. "Tomorrow's a workday, and I have to get up early."

Julia laughed, pushing them toward the front door. "Go on. You're starting to sound like a couple of high-school kids!"

As they drove away in Adam's pickup, he looked over and smiled. "Julia seems to be bearing up pretty well."

Susannah nodded, wondering again if he were aware of the rumors surrounding the circumstances of Josh's death. She decided to maintain her silence. If it was true, it was nobody's business but hers and Julia's; if not true, it was better to avoid the subject altogether.

She looked over at his strong profile, illuminated by the faint green lights of the instrument panel. "I've been thinking and thinking, Adam, and I don't know what to do about that job. I was so cocksure when I decided to run the company, so confident that I could do a good job. And now . . ." She sighed.

"Hush now." He smiled. "Let's forget the damned job for tonight, Susie. Tonight, all I'm interested in is *you.*"

"Me? Oh, Adam, you know all about me. You've known me since I was a pimply-faced high-school girl."

"You were never pimply faced, and I don't know a thing about the last few years." He looked over at her, a serious expression on his face. "What about men, Susie? Is there anyone special in your life right now?"

She thought about some of the men she had dated during her years in San Diego—navy officers, fellow civil servants—and compared them with Adam. None of them, in retrospect, measured up. "No. How about you?"

"Ah, well, I'm a kind of one-woman man, Susie. I've only loved two women in my life. The girl I married . . . and you. My wife is gone." He looked at her as he stopped the pickup at a traffic signal. "That leaves you."

"Adam, I—"

"Oh, don't worry," he broke in, cutting her off with a gesture. "I won't make a fool of myself." The signal changed, and he drove through the intersection, shifting smoothly through the gears. "One of the reasons I can be so open about it is that I don't figure there's a chance in hell of you and I ever getting back together. But you might as well know how I feel, right from the start. I'm not going to lie to you or try to fool you."

She was silent for a moment, looking out the window at the passing landscape, unable to be as open about her feelings as he was. She realized there were simply too many complicating factors at the present time.

"What was she like, Adam?" she asked, breaking the silence. "Your wife?"

"Ann?" He smiled slightly. "She was something, Susannah. You'd have liked her, I think. Ann was a perpetual optimist, always looking on the bright side . . . I was still just a manual laborer when I met her, but she believed in me, right down the line. When I got promoted, it was no surprise to Ann. To her, the company was just doing the right thing by her man. Annie was—she was a good person, Susannah."

"Was she pretty?"

"Yeah, she was pretty." He glanced over at her with a wry expression. "Not as pretty as you are, maybe, but pretty. Slim, brown hair, pretty eyes . . ." He swallowed, as if the memories were still painful, then looked back at the road.

"I'm glad you had somebody who made you happy, Adam," she said softly. "Ann sounds like a very nice person. I think I *would* have liked her."

"I loved her." He blinked rapidly a few times, then shook his head. "But life goes on. I've got Sheila to think about now, and as long as I've got her, well, a part of Ann is still with me. Can you understand that, Susie? Can you understand how a man can love two different women, and in different ways?"

"Of course I can. What you and I had . . . well, that was kid's stuff, I suppose. You and Ann lived as man and wife, had a child together. There's no comparison."

"No, there is no comparison," Adam said hoarsely, looking over at her again. "But that doesn't make what you and I had any less real, Susie. And it doesn't change the fact that you were my first love. There's always been a special place in my heart for you, no matter how things have changed between us . . . no matter what we've each become."

He laid his hand down on the seat between them, steering the pickup with his left hand. After a moment she reached over and put her hand on his. His fingers curled around hers, and for a moment they rode in silence. In spite of her misgivings Susannah asked the question that had been bothering her for several moments.

"Why—why don't you feel there's any chance of you and I getting back together, Adam?"

"Ah, Susie," he said, shaking his head, "I got the message years ago, when you dumped me while you were away in college."

"Adam, please," she remonstrated, squeezing his fingers. "Maybe that was more my fault than yours, but I was just a kid then, preoccupied with finishing college and very uncertain of of what I wanted to do with my life. Can you understand that?"

"And now?" He smiled bitterly as she hesitated. "See? I get the message. But don't worry, I'm not the kind of guy to slobber around somebody who doesn't want me." He smiled sadly. "But I would like us to be friends."

"Oh, Adam, of course we're friends. I hope we'll always be good friends."

They were silent for the rest of the drive to the restaurant. Susannah was pleased to see that he had selected one of the nicest steak houses in the area for their dinner.

Inside, the hostess showed them to a secluded table next to a window, overlooking a rock garden with a small fountain that was illuminated by strategically located spotlighting. Adam ordered a carafe of red wine and poured them each a glass. In the flickering candlelight, the wine sparkled like liquid rubies as they clicked their glasses together.

"To a happy life," Adam toasted.

"A happy life," Susannah murmured, then took a sip of her wine.

For a few moments they chattered about inconsequential matters, each avoiding anything serious, and Susannah felt herself beginning to relax. By the time the waiter had come and taken their orders for steak and lobster, she was feeling better than she had all day. *To hell with the job*, she thought inwardly. *Adam's right, tonight's for relaxing and enjoying ourselves.* They drank another carafe of wine with their meal, and by the time the waiter had removed their plates, they were feeling mildly inebriated, their stomachs pleasantly filled with good food and wine. Susannah realized she hadn't enjoyed a man's company so much in years.

"See that guy over there?" Adam asked quietly, indicating a thin, completely bald man seated a few tables away. "He tests toupees for a wig company in Los Angeles."

"Really? How do you—" She caught the mischievous expression in his eyes and laughed, remembering the game they used to play. Looking around the room, she spotted an enormous woman seated across the room from them. The woman was devouring a large steak, her jaws working rapidly, as if she feared that the waiter was hovering nearby to snatch the meat away.

"See that lady over there?" she whispered, pointing surreptitiously. "Her job is wear testing designer jeans."

Adam snorted with laughter, causing her to giggle. They spent the rest of their time there amusing each other with ridiculous remarks about their fellow diners, and Susannah was almost sorry when Adam groaned with repletion and pushed his chair back from the table.

"Oh, boy, I've got to loosen my belt after a meal like that. I always manage to make a pig of myself when I come here."

Susannah looked up, startled. "What did you say?" she asked, something skittering on the edge of her mind, something she knew was important.

"I just said I always overeat when I come here."

"No, before that!"

"I said I had to loosen my belt. Why?"

"I—I don't know," she said slowly, "but something is trying to come to me, Adam. Something important, maybe."

"Well, maybe it's that we'll all have to take our belts *in* if we don't come up with some work we can get financing on, and soon." He picked up the bill the waiter had left a few moments ago and studied it, then dropped some bills on the table. "Ready to go?"

"Yes." She stood, feeling strangely deflated and let down. Walking beside Adam, she found herself for some reason thinking about her first few moments in her father's office that morning. It had been so familiar to her, and yet . . . there had been an unfamiliar element, something new among the girlie calendars and snapshots. A calendar with a picture of a vast, open-pit mine, and—

"Adam!" she shrieked, just as he was opening the door of the pickup for her. "I've got it! I know what Dad had in mind for the San Gabriel Canyon job! I know how we can move that muck out of there a lot cheaper than with trucks!"

"How?" he asked skeptically.

"Belts! We'll do it with conveyor belts! That's what I've been trying to think of." She stared up at him, her eyes shimmering with happiness. Impulsively she stood on tiptoe and kissed him on the mouth. "Oh, Adam, we'll be all right now!"

He stared at her for a moment, a stunned expression in his eyes as she smiled up at him. Slowly he wiped his lips with the back of his hand, then before she had time to react or protest he crushed her in his strong arms, and his warm, firm mouth came down and covered hers. She struggled for only an instant, then surrendered to the delicious tingles radiating throughout her body from his kiss. Her lips parted, almost of their own volition, and she gasped in surprise and delight as his tongue slid into her mouth, probing, seeking, triggering sensations that made the backs of her knees feel weak and watery. She felt his big, demanding hands beginning to cup her breasts, and although she was almost completely without a will of her own, she stopped him with a startled gasp.

"No! Adam, please . . ."

Releasing her, he stepped back, a stunned, bewildered expression on his face. He raised his hands and looked at them, and opened his mouth in surprise when he saw they were trembling.

"I—I'm sorry," he said hoarsely. He drew a deep, shuddering breath, then gave a shaky little laugh. "I guess I don't have myself under such good control after all, Susie. Maybe it would be best if I just stayed away from you altogether."

She sagged as his hands left her, and if she hadn't reached up and caught the edge of the pickup door, she would have fallen. Adam walked quickly around to his side of the pickup while she stood there, feeling the strength and control gradually seeping back into her limbs. As she climbed up into the cab and leaned back against the seat, still breathing hard, she knew one thing for certain: The *last* thing she wanted Adam McBride to do was stay away from her . . .

CHAPTER FIVE

Adam pushed the sheaf of plans back, then switched off the clip-on lamp that stretched above the surface of the drafting table. As he stepped out of the tiny, partitioned room into the main part of the office trailer, he plucked his white hard hat from a hook near the door and placed it firmly on his head. Ed Highsmith, a studious-looking, bespectacled young man who seemed to wear a perpetual frown, glanced up from his calculator and nodded as Adam stopped in front of his desk, which sat just inside the door.

"Any word from the yard?" Adam asked.

"Yeah, Fran Parker called about an hour ago. She said Miss Lockwood herself would be delivering the checks, probably right after lunch."

"Thanks, Ed." Adam glanced at his watch as he reached for the doorknob. "That'll give me time to check everything with Ralph before she gets here. She'll want the grand tour."

"Well, she's the boss, I guess," Ed replied stonily.

"I'll be in my truck if you need me." Adam jerked his chin toward the two-way radio that sat on the counter adjacent to the timekeeper's desk. "You've been all checked out on that thing? Know all the call signs?"

"Of course I know how to use the radio," Ed muttered, his frown momentarily deepening. "And the call signs are taped to the counter."

"Okay, then. See you later."

Outside in the bright sunshine, Adam climbed into his pickup and started down the line of conveyor belts. The belt line passed behind the office trailer, which had been placed just a few yards off the state highway, and continued for almost three miles up into the canyon to the fill area. In the opposite direction the belt crossed under the road and stretched a half mile down toward the dam, where the excavation pits had been set up.

Glancing into his rearview mirror, Adam frowned, making a mental note to arrange for the water truck to make a pass along the graded dirt road; his pickup was throwing up a yellow-ochre trail of dust. They didn't want problems with the county dust abatement officials, not when everything seemed to be going so smoothly. The pickup's engine was inaudible as he drove down the smooth road; the conveyors running at full capacity just a few feet away, parallel to the road, were creating such a din it was impossible to hear anything else.

Adam felt a deep sense of contentment as he watched the sand and rock traveling up the canyon on the six-foot–wide heavy rubber belt at a steady ten miles an hour. At the present rate, he'd calculated, they would meet and exceed their stipulated goal for tonnage well before the end of the month. *Susie was right*, he thought proudly. *This is the only way to go.*

Slowing, he spotted Ralph Whitman's company pickup parked near the number one grizzly, a large framework that separated the boulders and other debris from the sandy material before it fell through onto the conveyors for its journey up the canyon. There was a grizzly, named for the huge steel teeth that were placed about eight inches apart, at each of the two pits that branched out from the end of the main belt line. Behind each grizzly, the pit—the area from which the soil was actually being removed—stretched in a fan shape for perhaps two or three hundred yards. Three huge D-9 Caterpillar tractors with oversized U-dozers attached worked each pit, gradually shaving the earth down to bedrock level, pushing the material up to the belt that fed the grizzly, then backing away for a new load.

There was one more necessary component to each

pit, the 966 Caterpillar rubber-tired loader, which sat in front of the grizzly, its diesel engine constantly idling, poised to clear any obstructions from the grizzly's teeth. The loader operator used an electronic device similar to a garage door opener to stop the short belt feeding the grizzly whenever a log or boulder stuck between the steel teeth of the grizzly. He would then clear the obstruction before starting the line running again. In this manner continuous, smooth operation of the belt line was possible.

Adam pulled to a halt a few yards in back of Whitman's pickup. Ralph Whitman was standing on the bottom steel rung of the 966 loader, talking to its operator. He glanced around, gave the operator a slap on the shoulder, then swung down and hurried toward Adam, wearing a broad, happy grin.

"Hey, does this beat the hell outta using trucks, or what?" He spoke loudly in order to be heard above the cacaphony of the equipment and the pounding of rocks against the grizzly.

"At the rate we're going, we'll have this canyon cleaned to bedrock by next September," Adam replied. He leaned down, peering out through the window, as one of the D-9's reached the grizzly belt with its load of sand and rock. "Talk about a skate job for those catskinners," he said with a wry grin. "Look at that damned blow sand—a good fifteen feet of it. Hell, there's hardly even a good-sized pebble to rattle their tracks! Why didn't *I* ever land on a gravy train like this when I was running equipment?"

"Well, yeah, but it has its drawbacks," Ralph replied soberly. "Some of the guys are starting to bitch about the noise."

"What?" Adam exclaimed, then grinned wryly as he saw the twinkle in Ralph's eye. "Seriously, how's it going?"

"Hell, couldn't be better—at least, so far. The company should really clean up on this job, Adam." He turned away for a moment, looking up at the pit area behind the grizzly as one of the D-9's approached, huge engine screaming as the dirt fell away from the gleaming blade of the U-dozer. "Y'know, I almost hate to pass this on," he said soberly, turning back to face Adam, "but I'm hearing rumbles about union again."

"Union? Come on, Ralph, our guys have turned the unions down twice in the last year."

"Yeah, *our* guys," Ralph agreed glumly, "but some of the extra help we had to put on for this job might be trying to stir up the boys, if you know what I mean."

"Yeah, I know what you mean." Adam thought for a moment. "Well, you know the law. They can talk union all they want—on their own time." He glanced up sharply for emphasis. "And that includes their lunch breaks, Ralph. Handle this with kid gloves—the last thing we need is labor trouble."

"Hell, you know me. I don't give a damn what they talk about, as long as they're doing their jobs. If they want to blow off a lot of hot air about unionizing, that's up to them." He shrugged. "But old Highpockets might—"

"You just pass the word to Highpockets," Adam interrupted sharply, frowning at the mention of Charles Schmidt, the long-legged, peppery night shift foreman. "If he has a problem with it, I'll take it up with him personally. Listen," he said, changing the subject, "Susannah's bringing the paychecks up right after lunch. She'll want the grand tour, so be sure your ducks are all in a row, okay?"

"No problem." Nodding, Ralph turned and walked toward his own pickup. Adam put his truck in gear and turned around and headed back toward the office, cursing mildly as he realized he'd forgotten to mention the dust problem. Plucking the microphone of his CB radio from the dash, he thumbed it. "Willy One to Willy Two." When Ralph acknowledged, he made his suggestion. "Ralph, how about having the water wagon make a pass or two along the access roads before you shut down for lunch?"

"Will do. Out."

Adam continued toward the office at reduced speed, thinking about Susannah's impending visit with a troubled frown. Their relationship had been progressing toward a new, more intimate phase during the past few weeks, but something always seemed to hold Susannah back at the last moment, spoiling everything and leaving him frustrated and angry at her and himself. He shook his head, remembering the weekend they'd spent in Arizona, when they'd flown to negotiate for the miles of conveyor belt needed for the job. They'd returned to the motel after a long session with Talman, the mine owner's representative, and gone to her room to go over the figures and discuss their progress . . .

"Oh, Adam," Susannah had exclaimed, her deep-blue eyes sparkling with enthusiasm, "it's going to work. I just know it is!"

"If it does, it'll be thanks to you," he said, gazing at her. He sat on the edge of the bed, watching while she paced the floor. In spite of his fatigue she had never looked as desirable, and the need to take her in his arms was almost more than he could bear. "Talman liked you —I could tell. If he signs, it'll be because of you."

"He would never have agreed to even see me without you." She came over and sat down on the bed next to him, taking his hand and squeezing it warmly. "But with you along, it was different. You have quite a reputation in construction circles, Adam. You're known as a man who can get the job done."

"We do make a good team, don't we?" He turned and looked into her eyes, and the moment changed for both of them. Her eyes widened a bit, then turned dark and smoky with desire as he drew her into his arms.

"Oh, Susie, you must know how I feel about you . . ."

Her lips were warm and soft as they yielded to him, and when they parted to allow the entry of his tongue, he gasped in delight. For a long moment they held each other, his desire for her becoming more intense by the second.

"Adam," she whispered as their lips parted. She leaned back, studying his face with an almost desperate intensity. Her eyes were wide as his lips came down on hers once again, and then they slowly closed as she groaned and melted against him.

Slowly he lowered her onto the bed, gathering her slender figure against him as their mouths moved together. He was trembling with need for her, pressing his body against hers as his hands found and cupped her firm breasts, her own hands busy on his chest, his neck, his firm shoulders.

"Susie, I need you." His hand slid down her thigh, tugging at the hem of the skirt she'd worn to the meeting with Talman, feeling the cool, smooth softness of her thigh as he raised the skirt. "Ah, baby, how I need you . . ."

"No, Adam, we can't!" She twisted away as his searching hand found the elastic band of her panties. Desperately she gripped his hand, pushing it down and away while she slid across the bed, away from him. "I—I—we just can't."

"Why, dammit?" he groaned, passing a hand over his eyes as she rolled away and got to her feet. "I love you, Susie. I need you. I want you. It's not as if we haven't done this—"

"We were different people then," she said harshly, cutting him off with a gesture. "We've got to find out who we are *now* before—"

"Before *what?*" he demanded, sitting up on the bed, frustrated and angry. "Dammit, Susie, I'm too old to play these games! We're not teen-agers anymore, and cold showers are not my idea of a good time."

She stood a few feet away from the bed, still trembling visibly. She looked at him with an expression of yearning in her eyes, then looked quickly away.

"Please, Adam . . . just leave me for a while. I need to think, and I can't while you're—while you're sitting there like that."

"Well, it's your fault I'm like 'that,'" he shot back,

drawing a deep, shuddering breath. "Just give me a minute, and I'll go back to my room."

She looked at him, a sparkle of mischief appearing in her eyes. A smile began forming on her lips. He felt himself responding to the humor of the situation, and when he reluctantly grinned, she burst forth with a peal of laughter. After a moment, he joined in.

"I'm sorry, Adam," she gasped after a few seconds, tears streaming down her cheeks. "It's just—" She collapsed again, hooting with laughter while he grinned ruefully. "Believe me," she said, calming down at last, "it's no easier for me. It's just . . . you'll have to give me time, that's all. I'm just not ready for—"

"I know," he broke in, able to get to his feet at last. "And I'll try to understand, Susie." He shook his head warningly. "But if you're going to kiss me like that, it's not going to be easy."

"We'll just have to watch ourselves," she said, her eyes still bright with amusement. At the expression of confusion that crossed his face, she added contritely, "Adam, I know it's not easy, but give me time. Please?"

And time's what I've been giving her, he thought grimly as he drove back toward the project office. He hadn't pressed, since that time in Arizona, but he was only human. A frown crossed his face as he remembered the piece of news he had to give her today. It could set their relationship back, and he wasn't looking forward to that, not one bit . . .

Susannah cranked her window wide open as she guided the Corvette up the winding mountain road, inhaling deeply the warm, fresh mountain air that felt so delicious against her face and skin after the long, wet, cold winter. She felt good today. The Williams Dam job had finally gone into full production the previous Monday, after more than three months of feverish preparation work, and it was already beginning to look as if her inspiration was going to pay big dividends for the company.

With a sense of satisfaction her hand dropped to the thick manila folder containing the weekly paychecks that lay on the passenger seat, across the console. Her employees, instead of being in danger of being laid off from their jobs, were working steadily, prospering, and earning overtime pay, and from the look of things, would continue to do so for the next year and a half. They'd even hired several extra hands in order to go into twenty-four-hour a day production; so it looked as if the expansion of the company she'd anticipated was well under way.

"And how about *that*, Mr. Banker McGruder?" she murmured aloud, smiling as she took a curve, the low car hugging the road in spite of her speed. "Is *that* good business or not?"

Adding to her sense of contentment was the manner in which her relationship with Adam was proceeding. They'd spent many long hours together during the past three months. The trip to Arizona together had brought a new warmth and depth to their relationship, bringing them to a plateau on which they'd been coasting now for several weeks. *Perhaps it's time for us to take the next step*, she thought, her pulse quickening.

Her feelings for Adam had been growing more rapidly than she would have thought possible, in spite of the fact that she was still troubled about the elusive agreement he claimed to have made with Josh. She was beginning to hope that perhaps they could grow into some kind of permanent relationship. If only he'd never mentioned the agreement, it would have all been so simple. It would have been wonderful to surrender to him, to let him carry them both off into the kind of ecstasy she knew they were capable of, to let him release the desire he'd been keeping such a tight rein on for so long now . . .

He'd been as good as his word, however, except for that one time over in Arizona, never pressing for anything beyond the simple pleasure of being with her. They'd been to movies, dinner, dancing; once they'd gone to Los Angeles to see the currently popular stage musical to which tickets never seemed available to ordinary mortals. How Adam had obtained them she never discovered. He'd been a perfect gentleman through it all, keeping his feelings under strict control. Her smile grew warmer as she remembered last Saturday night . . .

"Oh, Susie," he'd groaned as they parted from one of their long, deep kisses, which was as far as she'd been willing to go with him up until now, "I don't know how much longer I can go on like this." He looked at her with a rueful grin. "I've just about forgotten what it's like to take a *hot* shower."

If only he'd known, she thought, how difficult it had been for her to send him away all those times when her body cried out for him, for fulfillment, maybe he would have felt better about it. She'd had experience, of course —nobody knew that better than Adam. But she had learned that a casual approach to something as intimate as sex was not for her, and she didn't want to proceed any further with him until she had made up her mind about him once and for all. Carrying a torch for the man who had made her a woman was one thing; making a commitment to him, even if only in her own mind, was something else altogether . . .

The office trailer came into view, and she pulled off the highway into the graded area. Parking next to Adam's pickup, she pulled down her mirror to check her appearance before getting out of the car. She'd just had her hair cut, so the loose, natural curls needed no attention, other than to sweep the hair back from her face, where the wind had blown it. Susannah removed her sunglasses and studied her face, nodding with resignation after a moment. Her heavily lashed blue eyes required no assistance from cosmetics, but she had applied lipstick, wanting to look as appealing as possible today. She frowned at the light-brown spray of freckles across her nose; they always arrived with the warm, sunny weather, and there was nothing she could do about them. Adam claimed to like them, so perhaps she could consider them an asset. Her eyes brightened at the thought, and she decided to leave the sunglasses off for the moment. She glanced down at her clothes. She'd dressed for the occasion in tight-fitting tan jeans, boots, and a cobalt blue silk blouse that deepened the blue of her eyes and clung just tightly enough to the curve of her breasts. Satisfied, she stepped toward the door of the trailer.

"Uh—hello!" Ed Highsmith leaped to his feet as she entered the trailer, knocking a half-filled coffee cup to the floor in his haste. Blushing furiously, he quickly bent and scooped up the larger pieces. "I—uh—you *are* Miss Lockwood, aren't you?"

Susannah couldn't help laughing. "You must be Ed Highsmith," she greeted warmly. "Our new time-keeper, right?"

"Yes, ma'am, I mean—uh—miss—" His blush grew even darker as he groped for words, and she smiled reassuringly.

"You might as well call me Susannah, Ed. Everyone else around here does." She looked around expectantly. "Is Adam here?"

"Hi, Susie." Adam's deep baritone voice came from the doorway that led into the small cubicle where his drafting table had been installed. "Have a nice drive up?"

"Just beautiful," she replied, her eyes devouring him, reflecting that outdoor work was good for him. His tan had deepened several shades with the onset of spring, making his teeth look whiter, and the pale blue of his eyes seemed even more vibrant. "I was hoping you'd have time to show me around the job, Adam."

"Oh, I've always got time for you." He stepped closer, glancing at the folder under her arm. "Paychecks?"

"Yes. Do you take them?"

Adam casually took them from her, then handed them to the timekeeper. "Get these sorted out and give them to Ralph when he comes for them. Pull mine, and yours, of course, and be sure to leave the night shift's checks in Schmidt's box on the counter, or there'll be hell to pay on Monday." Turning back to her, he smiled. "Ready for the grand tour?"

"Ready and eager!" She took his arm and he escorted her out of the trailer, Ed Highsmith watching with wide, admiring eyes as Susannah passed in front of his desk. At the bottom step of the stairs she cocked her head and smiled. "Mmm! Just listen to that belt hum, carrying all that dirt up the canyon!"

"Something else, huh?" Adam grinned as he opened the passenger door of his pickup. "Better buckle up," he suggested as she slid onto the seat. "The road can get bumpy."

Obediently she pulled the strap across her chest and clicked it in place. "All set."

He glanced over as he switched on the ignition. "Do you want to start at the top or the bottom?"

"Right to the top," she said happily.

"You got it." He backed the pickup out of the small yard in front of the trailer, then headed up the canyon on the dirt road, which had been baked by the sun and the continual passage of trucks and equipment to the consistency of asphalt. The road ran parallel to the belt line, only inches away in some places, veering away only when the belt crossed a deep ravine on a temporary steel bridge, rejoining the belt line on the other side.

"The belt runners drive up and down this road all through their shifts, checking on the line," Adam pointed out. "Any sign of a pileup or a jam, they stop the line and clear the obstruction before any damage is done. At least," he finished with a grin, "that's the theory."

Susannah nodded, her eyes shining at the sight of all this machinery she had brought together and set in motion. It was a far cry from the paper shuffling that had been her job up until a few months ago . . . Suddenly she was reminded of a conversation she'd had with Fred Ward that morning. Fred had come into her office with a set of plans for another, smaller job to ask her advice on a minor technical matter, and they had ended up discussing the canyon job.

"Do you think Dad had belts in mind all along, Fred?" she had asked. "And if he *did*, why didn't he write the bid that way in the first place?"

Fred thought for a moment before replying. "I think he did plan to use the belts all along, Susannah. Probably wanted the job bid written the way it was to avoid tipping off the competition. Know what I mean?"

"So they wouldn't tumble onto the idea of using belts and adjust their bids accordingly?"

"Exactly." Fred had taken out a cigarette and lit it, dropping the match in the old piston ashtray on her desk. "He sewed up the job without letting on about his idea for using belts instead of trucks." As he exhaled a cloud of blue smoke, he coughed and waved a hand expressively. " 'Course, that's just an old man's guess, Susannah . . ."

Now, as Adam stopped the pickup at the fill area, she decided that Fred's guess was probably as close to the truth as they would ever get. As Fred pointed out, it was just a guess, but it was the guess of a man who had worked closely with Joshua Lockwood for over fifteen years. Anyway, she thought as she climbed down from the high seat, accepting the hand Adam offered, she'd proven, at least to herself, that she was enough of an engineer to design an efficient method of moving millions of tons of dirt.

"There it is," Adam said, gesturing toward the tall, portable conveyor belt on wheels. A steady stream of dirt poured from its tip, thirty feet above ground level. Two D-9 dozers were pushing the accumulated earth away from beneath the conveyor as quickly as possible, gradually building a smooth, level pad where there had been only a shallow gulch days before.

"The start of Williams Dam Recreational Park," Adam continued. "Two years from now, this'll be a beautiful, terraced park up here, and the property owners association will start recovering some of their cost for this job."

Susannah nodded absently, staring at the frantically working bulldozers, which were shoving the material away from the foot of the conveyor. "Are those two guys going to be able to keep up?"

Adam glanced over and nodded. "Sure, as long as they've just got that short push. We'll bring another rig or two up as needed, and when necessary we'll extend the belt to the next gulley."

"I'm just glad you're up here running things," she admitted slowly. "Seeing all this in action is a bit overwhelming, even if I did see it on paper first."

He grinned and gave her shoulder a squeeze. "Well, that's what you're paying me for. Seen enough?"

She nodded, and they got back into the pickup. Adam drove slowly down the belt line, crossing the road in front of the office trailer and continuing on down to the pits, which had been cut down by several feet since his visit earlier that day. Susannah asked several questions, all of which he answered with patience and thoroughness.

"What's going on there?" she asked as they drove back toward the office trailer. Adam looked in the direction of her pointing finger. On the other side of the belt line, in the cleared maintenance area, a D-9 was parked. The flickering light of an arc welder could barely be distinguished in the shade cast by the huge dozer blade.

"A loose trunion arm." Adam shrugged, dismissing it from his mind. "Bill's got one of his boys fixing it up."

"Trunion arm . . ." she murmured, wishing she hadn't asked. It seemed as if her ignorance increased in direct proportion to the amount of time she spent up here on the job site. "I think I'm ready to head back to the yard," she said faintly.

"Sure thing." He accelerated slightly as they started up the hill toward the office trailer. When he pulled in next to her Corvette, she reached for the door handle and started to get out. "Wait, Susie," he began, a vaguely troubled expression on his face. "I've got something I need to talk to you about, if you can spare another few minutes."

"Oh, couldn't it wait until tonight, Adam?" She smiled, putting her hand on his arm. "Speaking of tonight, how would you feel about eating at my place instead of going out? I'd like to cook for you . . . and I want tonight to be very special for us."

He stared at her for a moment, his eyes widening in comprehension as she smiled into his eyes. His troubled expression was suddenly erased by a broad, anticipatory smile.

"Yeah, that'll be fine, Susie. Tonight'll be fine . . ."

It had better be, Susannah thought that evening as she put the final touches on the dinner she'd prepared for the two of them. She stepped back from the counter, reviewing her efforts. The stuffed pork chops were ready to go into the oven; the salad was tossed and waiting in the refrigerator, and the potatoes were baking in the oven.

"Everything better be just fine," she murmured aloud. She looked around the interior of the condominium she'd moved into several weeks ago, over Julia's loud protests. The place was immaculate. The table in the dining area was set with her best china, linen napkins, and flatware, and two candles stood in gleaming brass sconces, awaiting the touch of a match. A bottle of good California Rhine wine was chilling in the refrigerator, and a fresh pot of coffee waited in its glass decanter on the hot plate.

Satisfied, she hurried into the bedroom, where she stripped off the clothing she'd worn to the office that day, then went into the bathroom. She enjoyed a long, luxurious soak in the tub, feeling the tensions of the day evaporating like the steam that rose from the surface of the water. After bathing and shampooing, she sat on the edge of her bed and dried her hair, then opened her closet.

The dress she'd purchased especially for this occasion hung in solitary splendor at one end of the closet—a soft, lacy blue silk that clung to her curves without being in the least tight or uncomfortable. The scooped neckline revealed just the right amount of cleavage, she noted with satisfaction, enticing and drawing the eye yet doing so within the confines of good taste. She pirouetted in front of the mirror, checking for threads or tags, then sat down in front of her dresser and applied a touch of lipstick. She wrinkled her nose, but the freckles remained exactly where they were.

With one last critical glance she slipped her feet into a pair of satin slippers. Before switching off the light she turned and inspected the bedroom. Like the rest of the house it was in perfect order: fresh sheets and pillow cases on the bed, the nightstands dusted and polished, and everything picked up and put away. After putting fresh towels in the bathroom she would be as ready as she would ever be. She attended to that detail, then went into the living room and switched the radio on to an FM station that specialized in soft, romantic music.

In the kitchen she put the stuffed pork chops in the oven, then poured a glass of wine and glanced at the clock. Adam was due in twenty minutes; the pork chops would be done in half an hour. *Perfect,* she thought.

His knock on the front door came promptly at seven thirty, just as the house was beginning to fill with delicious aromas wafting from the kitchen. His eyes widened in appreciation as she opened the door and gestured for him to come in.

"Wow," he breathed, leaning down for her kiss, "you get better looking every time I see you, lady."

"Thank you, kind sir." She looked him up and down, liking what she saw. He wore a loose brown sport shirt, his crisp, blond hair curling through the open collar, and a pair of tan slacks whose crease broke sharply over a pair of suede loafers. "You don't look so bad yourself."

As he lowered himself onto the small sofa, she asked, "Would you like a drink? I've got some beer, and I plan to serve wine with dinner. The food will be ready in about fifteen minutes."

"Sure, a glass of wine would be fine." Following her, he watched her move around the kitchen, entranced by the way her silk dress clung to her curves as she handed him a glass of wine. "Thanks."

"Here's to the successful launching of the canyon job," she toasted, raising her glass to clink against his.

"To the canyon job . . . and its engineer," he said huskily, then took a sip, his eyes never leaving her face. She stepped around him, walking back into the living room, where she sat down. Adam followed, sitting down next to her.

"How's Sheila?" she asked.

"Oh, she's just fine." He gave her a sly smile. "She's been putting me through the third degree about you, though." He shook his head ruefully. "Three years old and already worrying about her daddy."

"I can't wait to meet her. I hope she'll like me."

"She'll be as crazy about you as I am." Pausing, he took a sip of wine, then said, "How about coming over to my place for dinner this Sunday? I've been planning to take Sheila over to San Bernardino to watch model trains run, and you could join us. I might even take one of my trains along. What do you think?"

"That sounds fun, Adam." She turned on the sofa, smiling quizzically. "I didn't know you were interested in model trains."

"Miniature steam engines, not models," he corrected. "I build my own engines from scratch. It's a relaxing hobby."

The timer went off a few moments later, and Susannah rose to put the food on the table, glancing over at him as he sat on the sofa, leafing through a magazine, enjoying the domesticity of the scene. When she called him to the table, he raised his eyebrows in surprise.

"Candlelight and wine, eh?" He smiled. "Maybe Sheila *should* be worried about me."

Susannah was pleased with the way the meal turned

out. The stuffed pork chops were perfectly done: the meat was tender and delicious, and the stuffing was cooked to just the right texture. Adam wolfed down two of them, groaning with repletion as he finally pushed his plate away.

"Not only is she beautiful and capable of designing bridges—she can cook, too! Susie, that was the best meal I've had in a long time."

"Thank you." Absurdly pleased by his compliment, she quickly cleared the table, rinsing and stacking the dishes in the dishwasher. After refilling their wine glasses, she joined him on the sofa. "There's some pie for dessert, if you'd like."

"Maybe later. I'm pretty satisfied."

"How about some music?" She went over and knelt on the carpet in front of her stereo, sorting through her collection of records, which had been vastly enlarged by the ones Josh had left her. "I'm afraid most of this stuff is pretty old, Adam . . ."

"That's fine with me. I like the old stuff."

"Jimmy Dorsey okay with you?"

He brightened, and she knew he hadn't just been being polite. "Do you have 'So Rare'?"

Smiling, she slipped the album from its sleeve and put it on the turntable. "It's one of my favorites."

She sat back down beside him as the familiar music filled the air, feeling the usual tingle of delight as Jimmy Dorsey's clarinet soared along with the orchestra. When Adam's strong arm went around her shoulders, she tensed momentarily, then relaxed against his warm, firm body as naturally and easily as if they'd been lovers for years.

"It's good being here with you like this," he murmured, nuzzling her hair with his chin, sending little shivers of delight up and down her spine. "It feels right."

"Yes, it does," she said softly. "I feel as if I've really gotten to know you these past few weeks. I liked Adam the boy . . . but Adam the man is even better."

She glanced up, his strong chin filling her field of vision, and smiled. It was true. Working with someone on a day-to-day basis, observing how they met and overcame adversity of all sorts, brought a new depth of understanding and affection for that person. Everything she had learned about Adam during recent weeks had deepened her feelings for him.

"Adam the man, eh?" He turned and smiled into her eyes. "I suppose you know how this man feels about you?"

"I know, Adam," she whispered. "And I want you to know how much I appreciate the way you've respected my feelings. You've been more patient than I had any right to expect."

"And now?"

For an answer she turned her face up to meet his questioning lips, feeling a shimmering flood of joy spreading through her body as his tongue gently probed at her lips. Her lips parted, and as his tongue eagerly entered her mouth she gasped with pleasure, twisting on the sofa to give his searching hands better access to her body.

"Ah, Susie," he groaned, understanding that she was at last on the verge of surrender, "how I've waited for this!" He sighed happily as their mouths merged once again, and his hands traveled gently over her curves, caressing her breasts, gently stroking her hips, creating wave after wave of delicious sensations. His lips moved against the soft, sensitive skin of her neck and nibbled at her earlobe, sending lightning bolts of thrills up and down her body.

"Adam . . . I want you," she murmured, half groaning as he licked at her ear. She was half lying across his lap, weak with a delicious languor as he stroked her, wanting him so badly she ached with need.

She sighed as she felt his strong arms gather her up, laying her head against his broad, firm chest as he got to his feet and carried her toward the bedroom. When he gently lowered her onto the pillow, she looked up at him through half-closed eyes as he switched on one of the soft bedside lamps and gazed down at her adoringly.

"You're sure?" he asked hoarsely.

"Oh, yes, my darling," she breathed, "I'm sure."

He lay down beside her on the bed, gently kissing her throat as he began unbuttoning her dress. His eyes were dark with desire as he removed it and tossed it aside. She wore only panties and a lacy bra now, and he swallowed audibly as he looked at her for a moment. He reached for the catch of her bra, and she caught his hand, stopping him.

"Now you," she murmured, her eyes shining in anticipation.

Nodding with understanding, he began removing his clothing. He kicked his shoes aside, then unbuckled his trousers and stepped gracefully out of them. When he peeled his shirt off, she shivered at the sight of his well-defined, ridged stomach with its tracing of coarse, curly blond hair. He laid back down beside her, and she ran her fingers through the thick hair on his chest, crooning with pleasure while he gently unfastened her bra and removed it, bending over to kiss each erect nipple as he did. He cupped her breasts one by one, taking the nipples in his mouth and circling them with his tongue until the pleasure was almost unbearable.

"Now, Adam, now," she moaned, arching her back slightly to help him slide her panties down. As the wispy strip of fabric disappeared and his warm hand caressed the moist core of her being, she gasped with pleasure, moving involuntarily with short, thrusting motions, but still he held back, his loving sweetly agonizing.

"Hold on, baby," he whispered huskily against her throat. "I've been waiting for so long . . . I want our lovemaking to last for us. I want it to be perfect." He raised up a bit, looking into her eyes. "My God, you're beautiful!"

He lowered his head to her breasts, moving back and forth between them, tantalizing each tender, sensitive nipple, worshipping her body. Then, gradually, his moist lips and tongue traveled down her flat stomach, leaving an electric trail of delight, lower and lower, until she sobbed at the painful pleasure of what he was doing.

"Oh, Adam, I want you now! Now!" She pulled him back up to her, her hands clawing desperately at his lean hips, tugging at his shorts, slipping them down his thighs . . . She audibly sucked in her breath in pleasure as his firmness sprang free and rested hotly against the smooth skin of her thigh. "Oh, please," she moaned, "don't make me wait any longer . . ."

"Ah, Susie!" Moving over her, spreading her thighs with his knees, he hesitated for just another moment, gazing down into her face. She grasped him in her hand then, and he cried out in pleasure as she helped their bodies blend together at last. As they began to move in the timeless rhythms of love, their pleasure mounted higher and higher, growing dizzyingly intense—a series of waves breaking on the soft, white yielding sands of a deserted beach. When their pleasure finally crested and burst like white foam against sheer dark cliffs, they cried out as one in the sweet, agonizing ecstasy of release . . .

She lay contentedly with her face resting against the warm, firm skin of his chest; although a wiry tendril of dark-blond hair was tickling her nose, she was too lazy and relaxed to move. He spoke, creating a low bass rumble in her ear, and she snuggled a little closer to his warm, muscular body, sighing happily.

"Hmmm?"

"I said this might be a bad time to bring it up, but have you had any luck looking for Josh's copy of the agreement between him and me?"

Her mood abruptly spoiled, Susannah sat up and stared down at him. Shifting uncomfortably, he hitched himself up on one elbow, a wary expression on his face.

"No, Adam, I haven't," she said flatly. "I've gone through several boxes of his papers and stuff from the office, but I haven't found anything. Why?"

"Well, I'm in kind of an awkward position . . . You see, I've been approached by Beck and Gray International with an offer for a hell of a good job in South America. The pay—well, it would be fantastic, and I could take Sheila along with me." He paused, then took a deep breath. "I have to give them my decision by the first of September, Susie."

"I see," she answered coldly, wondering how much of what had just happened had been for the purpose of warming her up, making her amenable to his demands. "But you'd turn it down, of course, if you suddenly became a partner in Lockwood and Sons?"

Adam looked away, and she stared at him in silence for a moment. She sighed as everything that had been troubling her about him rose up fresh in her mind, as if it had been lurking just out of sight while they pleasured each other, waiting to spring up and spoil her mood.

I love him in spite of all my doubts, she thought with a sensation of surrender that came as a tremendous relief. Whether he lied to her or Josh had lied to him no longer seemed to matter quite as much in view of what had just taken place between them. And if a tiny part of her mind continued to nag at her, questioning his character, well, it would stop eventually . . .

"Adam, have you—have you ever considered remarrying?"

He glanced sharply at her. "Are you suggesting that I marry you, become a partner in the company that way?"

"There could be worse things, couldn't there?" She placed a hand on his arm, eager for him to accept, trying to quiet the persistent uneasiness in her mind. Surely her love would be powerful enough to overcome her doubts. "You would become an equal partner."

"Thanks, but no thanks." His mouth flattened into a thin, obstinate line. "I'll be an equal partner *when* I marry, not because of it. Dammit, honey, don't you see? I couldn't ask you to marry me, not the way things stand now. I'm a nobody, with hardly a dime in the bank, and you're the owner of the company."

"What's the difference?" she demanded angrily. "If Dad wanted to make you a partner—"

"*If?*" Abruptly he got to his feet, furiously tugging on his clothing, his face a stubborn, angry mask of resistance. "You've *never* believed me, right from the start, have you?" He glared at her as he stepped into his shoes. "I'm *not* a liar, no matter what you've been thinking!"

"Adam, wait!" she exclaimed as he stalked out of the room. She grabbed a robe from her closet, following him toward the front door, appalled at the way the evening was turning out. He stopped with his hand on the doorknob as she yelled, "Well, Adam, it's beginning to look as if *somebody*'s been lying!"

"And that automatically makes it me, I suppose?" His eyes were dark with anger and misery. "Thanks for the dinner—and all the rest of it. It was great."

As the door closed firmly behind him, she stood in the center of the room, trying to choke back the tears. At last she gave a great, gulping sob and let them flow.

CHAPTER SIX

Susannah rose early the following morning and stood looking out her bedroom window at the spectacularly beautiful day: crisp, clear, blue skies and balmy temperature in direct counterpoint to her glum mood. Sighing, she dropped the curtain back into place, wishing that last night had ended differently.

After Adam's stormy departure, she'd spent the remainder of the night restlessly tossing and turning, replaying their conversation over and over in her mind, remembering just when everything had gone wrong. It had all been so lovely, so beautiful between them, but when Adam had reminded her of the agreement between himself and Josh, a chill had descended over the evening. *And that business about Beck and Gray International wanting to recruit him,* she thought with a trace of bitterness, *was the real capper. If Adam McBride truly believed that I would simply cave in and sign over a quarter of my company because of that sort of pressure, he was sadly mistaken.*

As she moved around the kitchen, reheating the coffee from last night and pouring a cup to drink before her shower, it occurred to her that she should have been expecting her anger instead of being surprised by it. For some time now the suspicion that Adam had lied about the agreement he claimed to have signed with Josh had been gnawing relentlessly at her subconscious, in spite of her attempts to suppress it. And when Adam rejected her not-quite proposal, which she had made in an attempt to eliminate the purported agreement as a factor in their relationship altogether, her anger had simply boiled over.

"Stubborn, stiff-necked fool!" she muttered, remembering his obstinate insistence upon clinging to his mythical 'right' to part ownership of the company.

Still, she had to admit that perhaps it was better this way. If Adam had eagerly accepted her proposal, she would always have wondered . . .

As she took another sip of the coffee, she sighed heavily. Adam *must* have lied. The alternative was an even more distasteful prospect: that the agreement had indeed been signed but that Josh had lied to Adam and had never intended to honor it when the time came. In either case a man she loved, respected, and admired had been lying through his teeth: her adored father, the standard by which she had always measured other, lesser men; or Adam, the embodiment of all that she desired in the way a woman desires a man. Idolized father, or the lover whom her body ached for in a way that was totally beyond her control.

"Time to grow up, little girl," she muttered wryly, tossing the dregs of her coffee into the kitchen sink. After rinsing the cup and placing it in the drainer, she went to the bathroom for her morning shower. *There has to be a logical explanation for this whole mess, but no matter what it is,* she thought, *one of my heroes will wind up with feet of clay.*

Forty-five minutes later, dressed in jeans and a light-blue sweater, Susannah left the condominium, heading toward Julia's place for what had, over the last several weeks, become their regular Saturday morning breakfast date. After parking the Corvette next to Julia's Eldorado, she entered the house after only a perfunctory knock to announce her presence.

"Morning." Dressed in a peasant blouse and a colorful rufffled skirt, Julia was seated at the table in the family room, frowning over the crossword puzzle from the morning newspaper. "Good heavens," she exclaimed, staring at Susannah in consternation, "what's happened to you? You look as though you haven't slept a wink!"

"Well, I didn't sleep very well, as a matter of fact." Susannah sat down across the table from Julia, reaching for a section of the newspaper. She opened it to the entertainment section and glanced disinterestedly at the selection of movies playing the local theaters. "Adam came over for dinner," she said after a moment. "We ended up fighting."

"A bad one?"

"Bad enough. We both said some things we probably shouldn't have."

"Hmm." With a sympathetic glance Julia got up and refilled her coffee cup, pouring a cup for Susannah as well. "They say the path of true love never runs smooth. You two probably wouldn't fight if you didn't care deeply for each other."

"Thanks." Susannah accepted the cup and took a sip, looking at Julia with a troubled expression. After a moment she asked, "Julia, did Dad ever say anything to you about some kind of agreement with Adam to give Adam a percentage of the company? Anything?"

Julia thought for a moment, then shook her head. "No, not that I recall. Why? Is it important?"

"No, it's nothing," Susannah said, shaking her head. She didn't want to lower Julia's opinion of Adam if it should turn out that he had been telling the truth.

"I drove up to the canyon yesterday to deliver the payroll and look the job over," she announced, changing the subject. "It's running like a Swiss watch, Julia. We're going to make a nice profit from the Williams Dam job, just you wait and see."

"That's terrific!" Julia beamed at her, and Susannah was grateful that she didn't seem to be wondering about her question of a moment ago. "Because of the belts, I assume?" When Susannah nodded, her smile grew even broader. "Well, you certainly showed them, didn't you? All those chauvinists who said a woman could never run a construction company. I'm proud of you, Susie."

"Well, we've got some pretty darned good people out in the field who make it all come together," Susannah admitted with a self-deprecating shrug. "I don't deserve all the credit."

"Still, you *are* the one who came up with the idea of using the belts." Julia paused a moment, then said, "I had some good news yesterday myself. The insurance company finally paid off on Josh's policy."

"And?" Susannah asked expectantly.

"They paid double indemnity," Julia declared with a triumphant smile.

"Oh, good." Susannah sighed audibly, a tremendous sensation of relief coming over her. "Then they really don't think—"

"It doesn't matter *what* they think," Julia interrupted firmly. "It means that they realize they could never prove how Josh died, that's all. I'm just glad it's over."

"How about you?" Susannah stared at her stepmother for a moment, waiting for a reply. "What do *you* think, Julia?"

"Listen, are you about ready?" Julia pushed the crossword puzzle aside and briskly got to her feet, a determined expression on her face. She picked up their cups and carried them over to the sink, speaking over her shoulder. "I'm taking you to the Red Lion in Ontario for their champagne brunch, since it's my turn to treat. I hear the food is just fabulous."

"Don't put me off, Julia," Susannah insisted. "What do you really think? Did Dad do it, or not?"

"Susie, I'm simply not going to think about that any longer." With a bright, false smile Julia took Susannah by the elbow and led her toward the front door, pausing to scoop up her keys and purse from the counter as they left the room. "I don't have to wonder anymore, so why should I keep torturing myself? Josh is gone. That's all that matters, and that's enough for me to deal with. I've been tearing myself apart wondering *why* long enough. No more. As far as I'm concerned, it's a closed subject. Savvy?"

"If that's the way you want it."

"It's exactly the way I want it," Julia declared. "It has to be." She got in behind the steering wheel of her car and switched on the ignition, revving the engine until it smoothed out. As she pulled the gear selector into reverse, she looked over and smiled. "I don't know about you, but I'm famished!"

During the fifteen minute ride to the Red Lion, Susannah found herself wishing that she could resolve the nagging questions surrounding her father's death so easily, but she realized she couldn't. She wouldn't be able to put it to rest until she knew, one way or the other, if her father had committed suicide. And if he had, why he had. The lingering guilt and anger that Julia was so obviously struggling against only fueled her determination; this good woman shouldn't have to suffer any further, and only the truth would make that possible. Without it Julia would always, in some deep recess of her mind, wonder if it wasn't somehow her fault that Josh was gone. As Julia steered the car into the vast parking lot at the Red Lion, Susannah pushed the troubling thoughts from her mind.

Inside the large, plush restaurant they lingered over large orders of eggs Benedict, light, fluffy biscuits, and a delicious white wine. In spite of all that was troubling her Susannah's appetite was whetted by the sumptuous breakfast.

"Tell me, how's your new job going?" she asked, sighing with repletion as she pushed her empty plate away.

"Oh, it's fun," Julia replied, smiling. "Teaching all those chubby little three- and four-year-olds the basics of modern dance is the most fun I've had in years. You should see them kicking up their heels and twirling around to the music. It's just about the cutest thing I ever saw . . . The studio doesn't pay very much, of course, but that doesn't bother me. I've got more than enough money, especially now. Having something useful and pleasant to do is more important than money."

Susannah smiled, trying to envision a room full of tots

struggling with the intricacies of modern dance. "I'll try to come by some afternoon, if I can get away from the office in time. Who knows, maybe I'll sign up for an aerobics class myself." Ruefully she eyed the remains of her breakfast, shaking her head. "A few more meals like this, and I'll sure need it."

"Ah, well, once a week you can splurge in good conscience." Julia chuckled as she opened her purse and took out money to pay the check. "Are you finished?"

Outside, the bright sunshine and rising temperature were forceful reminders that summer was just around the corner. Julia lowered the windows of the car as she started the engine and backed out of the parking space.

"How about some shopping?" she suggested as she drove slowly through the huge parking lot toward the exit. "I was thinking of going to the mall to look at some material for dancing costumes for the kids. Want to come along?"

"I'd love to," Susannah replied, "but I've got loads to do at the office."

"On Saturday?" Julia looked at her skeptically. "Come on, give yourself the day off. You are the boss, after all."

"I can't, Julia, but thanks anyway. I can get so much more done when the office is empty, without the phone interrupting me every few minutes. Just drop me off at the house so I can pick up my car, and you go ahead without me."

"All right." As Julia turned the car toward the exit, there was a set, almost angry expression on her face. She stopped at the entrance to the street, waiting for a break in the traffic, and glanced over at Susannah.

"You're going to spend the day going through your father's things, aren't you?" At Susannah's startled expression, she nodded wisely. "You're not satisfied. You're going to go on prying, pushing, sticking your nose into Josh's death until—until I don't know what!" She paused a moment, an almost vindictive gleam in her eye as she stared at Susannah. "Be careful, or you might uncover something you'd rather not know."

"I'll take my chances." Susannah met her stepmother's stare levelly, refusing to look away. After a moment Julia blinked several times, a suddenly vulnerable expression on her face, and looked away. Susannah's heart went out to the older woman, and she reached over and touched her on the arm.

"Julia, I want you to understand something. I don't think for a moment that Dad did what he did—*if* he did what I'm afraid he did—because of anything to do with you. He was always happy with you, happier than I ever knew him to be."

Julia just shook her head as she pulled out into the traffic and headed north, toward Upland. After a moment of silence she looked over at Susannah, her eyes moist with unshed tears. "I'm sorry for being hateful with you, Susie," she confessed, her voice breaking. "It's just—just that I've had a very difficult time dealing with what's happened, and now that the insurance company has dropped its investigation . . . well, I just have to let *go*, that's all. I can't see any point in digging any further."

"I understand," Susannah murmured. "Believe me, I do. But I have to know, Julia. I can't let it go, not yet."

They finished the drive back to Julia's house in silence, but when she stopped behind the Corvette in her driveway to let Susannah out, she reached out for her hand, giving it a quick, hard squeeze before releasing it.

"You do what you have to do, honey," she said softly. "We all have to deal with our grief in our own way, I suppose."

With a lump in her throat Susannah drove down to the yard and parked in front of the office trailer. As she unlocked the door, she glanced over at the maintenance shed, from which the whine of air wrenches and the mutter of welding machines were emanating. Bill Fredrickson's crew was busy almost all the time lately, keeping the equipment in shape for all the projects the company had under way in various locations.

Inside, the office trailer was quiet and empty, so she switched on the transistor radio she'd installed in her office a few weeks ago, humming along with the music of a golden oldies station as she pulled another of the cardboard boxes off the stack next to the filing cabinet and placed it on her desk.

Systematically she began sorting through the accumulation of advertisements, items of junk mail, odd notes, and scraps of paper with Josh's stiff, crabbed, almost indecipherable handwriting on them. As she worked, she wondered if her father had ever thrown *anything* away. Most of the stuff she tossed into the trash can, but she saved the few items she didn't understand for further study before disposing of them. This was the third of the boxes Fran had packed after Josh's death that she'd had an opportunity to look through, and she was beginning to doubt she'd ever find anything of importance.

"Dad," she muttered aloud, tossing another handful of advertisements into the trash can, "you were a real pack rat."

Uppermost in her mind as she worked her way through the accumulation of junk was anything resembling a formal agreement between Adam McBride and her father, but neither of the two previous boxes had yielded anything of the sort, and it was beginning to appear as if this one would not either. Almost at the bottom of the box, she sighed in disappointment as she lifted out a handful of glossy brochures from a tool company.

"Hey . . . what's this?" she muttered, tossing the ads into the trash can.

At the bottom of the box lay an imitation leather appointment calendar, several of its dog-eared pages falling from between the covers. From its condition she surmised it must be several years old, but when she opened it and checked the dates, she realized it was from the previous year. Her heartbeat quickened as she leafed through the pages until she came to last December.

"December twenty-eighth," she read aloud, "ten A.M., Doc 'C' . . . Doc 'C'?"

Rapidly she leafed through the tattered pages, discovering an almost identical notation every three or four weeks, dating back as far as the previous July. The last of the appointments, she observed with a pang of sadness, had been for a day less than a week before Josh's death.

Closing the notebook carefully, she placed it in her purse for further study. Intuitively she felt that there was a connection between the many appointments with the mysterious Doc C and her father's untimely death. Of course, she realized she could be jumping to an erroneous conclusion—she was assuming that Doc C was a medical doctor, and that whatever he was treating her father for had a direct bearing on his death, but she could be wildly off base. Doc C could be a dentist, for all she knew, or even a chiropractor; her father had visited a chiropractor whenever his back would flare up on him, which in recent years had been all too often.

Still, she felt strongly that she had discovered an important clue. She looked into the cardboard box, ascertaining that nothing important remained inside, then upended it into the trash can.

She sat down in the swivel chair behind the desk, drumming her fingers against the desktop, frowning in thought. If anyone was likely to know about the mysterious doctor, Fran Parker was that person. Taking her small address book from her purse, Susannah looked up Fran's home phone number, then pulled the telephone across the desk toward her.

"Fran? This is Susannah. Sorry to bother you on your day off, but—"

"Oh, that's okay," Fran interrupted cheerfully. "I was just watering my house plants. What can I do for you?"

Briefly she told Fran about the appointment calendar she'd found and asked her about Doc C.

"Gee, I don't know," Fran said slowly when Susannah was finished. "Josh was on the group medical plan, like the rest of the company employees, and I handled all his claim forms. But I sure don't remember any claims for a Dr. See."

"Not Dr. See," Susannah corrected. "Just Doc C—the initial *C.* Do you remember any doctors Dad saw whose names started with *C?*"

"No, I'm afraid I don't," Fran replied apologetically. "Josh usually saw Dr. Robinson, in the Upland Medical Building. Come to think of it, I made an appointment for him last spring sometime. In May, I think . . ."

"How about his dentist? Did you make his dental appointments for him?"

Fran laughed affectionately. "Oh, Lord, yes, and it was like pulling teeth to get him to go at all. He had to be practically dying before he'd let me call Dr. Peterson."

"Well, that eliminates the dentist, then. Do you happen to know what chiropractor he saw when his back was hurting?"

"No, I'm sorry, I don't," Fran said. "Our insurance plan doesn't pay for chiropractors, so Josh usually made those appointments himself, or maybe Julia did. Why don't you call her?"

"Good idea." Susannah had no intention of calling her stepmother, not after their conversation earlier that morning. "About that appointment for Dad in the spring—do you happen to know what it was for?"

"Oh, sure. It was just a routine physical. He had one every couple of years, of course." Fran paused for a moment, then added, "As far as I know, Susannah, that was the last time he saw a doctor. I'm positive it was the last time I submitted a claim form for him."

"Okay, then. Thanks a lot." On the verge of hanging up, Susannah caught herself, speaking quickly. "Still there, Fran?" She hadn't hung up yet, so Susannah said, "Fran, I've heard from various people that during the last several months Dad pretty much neglected the job.

That he wouldn't even come in for days at a time. If anybody knows the truth about that, it's you."

"Well, I . . ." Fran's voice was tinged with reluctance.

"It could be very important, Fran," Susannah prompted.

"It's just that I hate to speak ill of the dead. But if it's really important, the answer is yes—and no. He did neglect his job, but it's not true that he wouldn't come in to the office for days at a time. He was there almost every day, but he'd just sit at his desk, and he usually left before lunch. He never told me what he was doing or where he was going. I could tell something was eating at him, but—" She broke off, giving a sad, nervous little chuckle. "Believe me, Susannah, it didn't make things very easy for me. The foremen would call in with questions I couldn't answer, needing decisions I couldn't make . . . it got to the point that Adam was practically running things single-handedly during the past few months. If it hadn't been for him, I don't know what would have become of Lockwood."

"Fran, why haven't you told me about this before?" Susannah demanded, surprised and confused by the revelation that Adam had indeed been telling the truth, at least in part, about his role in the company during the past year.

"Like I said, Susannah, I hate to speak ill of the dead. And Josh . . . well, I've always thought the world of him. Besides," she finished stoutly, "he *did* finish up the bid for the Williams Dam job, didn't he? So what if he let some of the routine stuff slide for a while? He *deserved* to take it easy," she said, beginning to sniffle. "If he'd taken a long vacation, like I tried to convince him to do, maybe he'd—"

"I know, Fran, I know," Susannah comforted gently. "I didn't mean to upset you. Thanks for your help. Have a good weekend, and I'll see you Monday."

After replacing the receiver, she sat for a few minutes, then reached for the telephone book and looked up the number of Dr. Robinson's office.

"Doctor's office, Janet speaking. May I help you?"

"I'd like to speak briefly to Dr. Robinson, please. My name is Susannah Lockwood."

"Do you have an appointment, Miss Lockwood?" Janet's voice had cooled several degrees.

"No, I don't. I was hoping to just speak very briefly with the doctor, if I may. I—"

"Doctor's time is extremely valuable," Janet interrupted tersely. "Unless this is an emergency, you'll have to make an appointment."

"Look, uh, Janet," Susannah explained, "I don't need to see the doctor for a medical problem. I'd just like to ask him some questions about my father, who was a patient of his."

"Name?"

"My father? Joshua Lockwood." In the background she could hear the chatter of a computer keyboard, followed after a few seconds by a high-pitched beep.

"Yes, we have him," Janet confirmed, a trace of smugness in her voice. "I show a balance due of forty-three dollars and seventeen cents."

"Send a bill to his residence and it will be paid," Susannah said, beginning to grow impatient with the faceless bureaucrat on the other end of the line. "I didn't call to discuss his bill. I want to ask the—"

"You said 'was' a patient of ours? Is your father deceased, Miss Lockwood?"

"Yes," she replied wearily, "he is."

"I see. And was he under treatment by our office at the time of his demise?"

"No, not as far as I know. He—"

"Hold, please"—Janet cut her off crisply—"I have another call."

Chafing impatiently, Susannah tried to ignore the syrupy canned music emanating from the earpiece but was afraid if she put the phone down she might miss Janet's return to the line.

"Still there, Miss Lockwood?"

"Yes, of course."

"I have an opening on Tuesday at four fifteen. Is that satisfactory?"

"Look, I only need a *minute*, for Pete's sake! May I just *speak* to the doctor? If he's with a patient, I'll wait until he's free."

"Doctor is *never* free, Miss Lockwood," Janet icily informed her. "Furthermore, Doctor is not in this afternoon. If you must speak to him, it will have to be on Tuesday at four fifteen."

"Okay, fine. Make the appointment."

"It will be fifty-five dollars for the initial consultation, Miss Lockwood, and payment *is* expected at time of service. Doctor's time—"

"Yes, I know," Susannah interrupted wearily. "Doctor's time is extremely valuable. I'll be there Tuesday."

She replaced the receiver and stood up, suddenly eager to escape the close, confining atmosphere of the office. The peculiar, stilted conversation with Dr. Robinson's receptionist had been frustrating, and she was filled with gratitude for her excellent health. *What must it be like,* she wondered, *for a truly ill person to have to deal with a dragon like Janet?* Shaking her head at the thought, she walked out toward her car, inhaling the fresh, warm air. Just as she reached for the door handle, Adam's pickup rolled into the yard. He drove over and stopped next to the Corvette. For several seconds he sat behind the steering wheel, gazing at her with an unfathomable expression, then he shut off his engine and got out and walked over to her.

"I figured you'd be here," he began in the low, husky baritone voice that never failed to send shivers up her spine. "I tried calling your place, then Julia's, then tried to call here, but the damned line's been busy for ages."

"I know." She gestured awkwardly, suddenly feeling shy and uncertain of herself. How was it that his mere presence had the power to turn her into a fumbling, mawkish schoolgirl? She swallowed dryly as she looked up at his tanned face, leaning against her car to steady her suddenly wobbly knees. "I've been on the phone."

"Yeah, that's probably why it was busy," he returned with a faint, ironic smile. "Listen, Susie, I—"

"Adam, I—" she said at the same moment. They looked at each other and laughed, and she suddenly felt much more comfortable and relaxed. "You go first," she insisted.

"Well . . . I just wanted to apologize. I'm sorry about last night." He stared at her with those compelling light-blue eyes, and she shivered, as if he were peering knowingly into the very depths of her soul. She warmed under his gaze, and only with an effort did she resist the impulse to throw herself into his arms. Her reason told her to proceed with extreme caution around this man— he might be a liar and a cheat—but her body continually betrayed her with its hunger for him.

"About . . . last night?" she asked weakly.

"You know." He shrugged awkwardly, spreading his big, powerful, bronzed hands. "I know it must have seemed like I was pressuring you, telling you about the offer from Beck and Gray. Susie, that was the last thing I intended."

"Forget it, Adam," she heard herself saying, to her dismay. "I was out of line, too."

"No, you weren't," he said miserably, looking away. "I've been thinking about that. And I want you to know something, Susie. It's not because I don't love you that I—"

"Look, Adam," she interrupted, a note of desperation in her voice, "why don't we both try to forget what happened last night? We both got carried away and said some things we shouldn't have, things that would have been better left unsaid."

"Yeah? Like what?" he demanded, his eyes blazing with intensity. His hands came up and gripped her shoulders, and she trembled from his touch. "Like when you said you loved me? Or when I said I love you?"

"Adam, I . . ." She shook her head in confusion, desperately trying to organize her thoughts. She'd had everything all figured out, and he had to come along and—*and just exist*, she realized with a start of surprise—and all her carefully thought out plans evaporated into thin air. So much seemed to be happening, and so quickly. "I think that we should slow down a little. Yes, I said I love you, and I don't take it back now. I'm—I'm happy that you love me, Adam. But there's just so much in our way right now!" She twisted out of his arms, sagging against the side of her car, breathing rapidly.

"Susie," he asked, *"are* you sorry about last night?"

"No, I'm not sorry. But I think we should cool it, at least until I—"

"Honey, you can't put the toothpaste back in the tube," he said gently, smiling lovingly into her eyes. "I waited for last night for months, and I'm not ready to go back to cold showers and empty beds. We're both adults, Susie. We love each other—we've already cleared that up. So why can't we have a physical relationship in the meantime, while you finish up whatever it is you have to do?"

She stared at him for several seconds, her thoughts and emotions in a quandary, then slowly shook her head. "I'm sorry, Adam," she whispered. "I can't. I just can't. I love you, but—"

"Yeah, like hell you do." Groaning, he turned away and yanked the door of his pickup truck open, standing there with his head bowed for a moment. "I warn you," he muttered hoarsely, "I won't wait forever. I'm only flesh and blood, Susannah, not whatever kind of superman it is you seem to be looking for!"

Without looking back again, he jumped into his pickup. The engine coughed and roared, and he sped out of the yard, the dual tires of the truck throwing gravel and dust high in the air.

CHAPTER SEVEN

Susannah was seated at her desk the next Monday morning, going over a stack of invoices, when her concentration was broken by the rumbling of a large diesel engine. She went to the small window and peered out into the gray fog, feeling a rush of dismay at the sight of a large semi and lowboy trailer pulling through the gate into the yard. Secured to the bed of the lowboy by thick steel chains and cables was the company's new D-9 Caterpillar tractor, looking oddly truncated, almost crippled, with its dozer blade and other attachments removed. Dropping the curtain back into place, she hurried back into the outer office.

"Do you know anything about that, Fran?" she asked, gesturing toward the open door. Outside, the truck was clearly visible as it pulled up and stopped in front of the maintenance shed a hundred yards away.

"No, I don't," Fran muttered, coming over to stand next to her at the open doorway. "Isn't that the new tractor he's got on that trailer?"

"It certainly is," Susannah confirmed, remembering the enormous monthly installment check she'd just signed on the tractor's purchase contract. "And they wouldn't be bringing it back down here from the Williams Dam job unless something was drastically wrong with it." She turned back to Fran with a grim expression on her face. "Get Adam on the line, will you?"

She was back in her office for only a moment before the soft buzz of her phone announced that Fran had obeyed her request.

"McBride here," Adam said crisply when she picked up the handset.

Although Adam certainly knew that it was she on the other end, his voice was cool and impersonal. Still, perhaps it was better that way. After all, wasn't that what she wanted? He had called her at home on Sunday morning to ask if she still planned to spend the day with him and Sheila, and she had regretfully declined. She wanted distance between them; that was what she had told Adam. *Why, then,* she wondered, *is his detachment now so painful to me?*

"I suppose you're wondering why the new D-9 has turned up on your doorstep, right?" Adam continued in the same cool tone.

"I certainly am. I thought that was our best tractor!"

"Was is the operative word." His voice was grim as he continued. "When the day shift operator fired it up this morning, it just quit on him. It ran for about fifteen minutes, then froze. Fredrickson took a look at it and recommended it be sent back down there for repairs."

"But why here? I thought they were supposed to be able to handle just about any repairs up there on site?"

"Sure, under normal circumstances, they can," Adam retorted. "But according to what Bill tells me, we might have a real serious problem on our hands. He *thinks* somebody dumped about ten pounds of sugar into the fuel tank, sometime between the time the night shift got off and the day shift took over. If he's right—and he usually is—we're looking at a major overhaul, and they can't do that up here. It has to be at the shop."

Susannah groaned, well aware of the enormous damage that a few pounds of sugar could do to an internal combustion engine. Sugar was mostly carbon, and when mixed with fuel and subjected to severe heat, it formed steel-hard deposits on all the internal moving parts of an engine.

"What do you think, Adam?" she asked glumly.

"Well, it's beginning to look as if we're going to have labor problems up here," he confessed with a sigh.

"Some of the newer hands are talking up the unions, and maybe some of our regular people have been influenced in that direction. But I'd be willing to bet a month's pay that none of our old hands pulled this off, Susannah. It has to be one of the new people, and most of them are on the night shift, under Highpockets."

"Do you think Highpockets is being too rough on them? If he is, that could explain the union talk and sabotage."

"I don't think so. He can be tough at times, but he's fair, and the men know it." He paused a moment, and when he continued, his voice had become hard and angry. "No, if we've got union agitators stirring things up, they don't need excuses for making trouble."

"But the men took a vote before that job got under way," Susannah protested. "They've had the opportunity to organize a union here several times, and they've always voted it down."

"Sure, I know that," Adam replied. "They don't want to give up steady jobs for a few cents more on their paychecks. They know when they're well off. If it came to a vote today, they'd vote against organizing. But some of the unions aren't too picky about the methods they use to influence people. And a company like Lockwood, which is just beginning to expand and bid on some sizable jobs, is a natural target for them. I'm afraid that sabotaging equipment is probably the least of the dirty tricks they've got up their sleeves." He paused, sighed, and then said, "It might be a good idea to think about hiring a security outfit to keep an eye on things up here. And it would probably be a good idea to have a guard posted down there at the yard, too, while you're at it."

"Maybe you're right," she replied thoughtfully. "But the expense!"

"The expense be damned," he retorted. "How much is it going to cost to rebuild that new D-9? If a security outfit could prevent just one more incident like this, they'd be worth every penny they cost."

"That's true . . ." She thought for a moment, then asked, "How long before Bill knows for sure if it was sugar in the fuel?"

"Oh, not long at all. When they get the compression head off that engine, it should be fairly obvious. Bill will let you know right away, one way or the other."

"All right, then. If that's what it was, I'll call in a security outfit—today. In the meantime, Adam, talk to the men up there and see what you can find out. If they have *any* valid complaints, act on them. Let's get this business defused as quickly as possible, before it blows up in our faces. And if you happen to find out who any of these bad apples are, I don't have to tell you what to do."

"You sure as hell don't." He chuckled mirthlessly. "They'll be off this job site within ten minutes." After a brief pause he said, "Was there anything else? I am sort of busy up here."

"I suppose that's all." She was oddly reluctant to sever this tenuous contact with him, in spite of all her resolve about putting their relationship on a more impersonal level until she'd found the answers to several unresolved questions. "I'll let you get back to work, then. Oh—do you want me to let you know about the D-9, when I find out?"

"Don't bother. Bill will be coming back up here this afternoon. He can fill me in."

She sat for a few moments after hanging up the phone, a wistful expression on her face. *If only I'd never heard anything about an agreement between Adam and Josh*, she thought, *everything would be so simple, so uncomplicated . . .*

With an effort she turned back to the stack of invoices, scrawling her initials in the corner of each one to approve payment. She held out a few, wanting further information before okaying them. She was just finishing up, ready to call Fran into her office to pick up the invoices and take them over to disbursing, when Bill Fredrickson appeared in her doorway. There was a grim, set expression on his blunt-featured, grease-streaked face.

"It *was* sugar?" she asked, her heart sinking.

"Yep." He pulled an oily rag from the hip pocket of his overalls and wiped his hands, frowning at the black half-moons of grime embedded beneath his fingernails. "Sure as hell was, Susie. I reckon I don't have to tell you that rig's gonna have to be torn right down to the bare block and rebuilt." Shaking his head, he swore under his breath for a moment. "Excuse my French," he muttered, "but if I could get my hands on the dirty SOB that done that, I'd—well, I'd wring his damned neck. That engine don't have three hundred hours on it yet!"

"And that kind of damage isn't covered by the guarantee, either," Susannah observed resignedly.

"Sure ain't. Comes under the headin' of deliberate abuse. Nope, we're gonna have to eat the expense of fixin' it back up."

"Well, do what you have to, Bill." She sighed, visualizing winged dollar bills vanishing into the sky. "Spend whatever you have to, to get it back on the job. It's costing us a lot of money every hour it's not working."

He nodded. "Yeah, well, I might be able to save quite a bit, Susie. But it's gonna have to have new gaskets and seals . . . probably new rings and bearings, too." Pausing, he pulled a cigarette from his pocket and stuck it into the side of his mouth, eyes squinted in thought. He exhaled a cloud of smoke and peered earnestly at her from beneath his bushy eyebrows. "You know this probably ain't gonna be the last one, don't you?"

"It damned well better be," she declared grimly. "I'm going to have armed guards on that job site by tonight, with orders to arrest anyone caught tinkering with our equipment."

"Well, now, that's what I was hopin' to hear." Fredrickson's face was split by a wide, relieved grin. "I don't mind workin' on 'em, Susie, but I'd sure hate to think I was just bashin' my head against a brick wall." He got to his feet, still smiling. "I reckon I'd better get busy, if I want that rig back on the job sometime this week."

"I have a lot of faith in you, Bill."

After Fredrickson left she spent the remainder of the morning on the telephone, interviewing security agencies based in the San Gabriel Valley. She took a break at lunch, leaving the office to find that the morning fog had been burned off by bright, hot sunshine. She cranked the sunroof of her Corvette open before driving away from the yard.

When she returned from lunch, she picked up where she had left off, working her way through the section of the phone book listing security agencies. She finally decided on an outfit called Special Security Systems, impressed by her conversation with the owner of the company.

"All our boys are ex-marines or soldiers, Miss Lockwood," Ed Bushnell told her. "Most of 'em have combat experience, and they're all fully trained and licensed in the use of firearms."

"I don't want anybody *shot*, Mr. Bushnell," she protested.

"Well, now, we've never shot anybody yet," he replied with a gravelly chuckle. "But we've made some pretty good arrests. If you check with the local police departments, I think you'll find we have a pretty good reputation in this valley."

"Arrests? What sort of arrests?"

"Well, we busted some guys who'd been stealing lumber and other building materials from a construction site we'd been contracted to protect, for one. And the owners of the big truck stop on the freeway just outside of town, they hired us to help control the drugs and whor— er, the prostitution that was going on, on their property. We worked with the cops on that one and got some pretty good busts, if I say so myself. Yep," he continued proudly, "our boys are all trained in powers of arrest and so on, so they won't get themselves—or you—

into legal troubles. You won't have to worry about that angle."

"I'm impressed, Mr. Bushnell. I guess my only remaining question is if you can have some men on our job sites by tonight?"

"No problem, Miss Lockwood. I'll come over to your office as soon as we hang up, go over the costs and so on with you, and get your John Henry on one of our standard contracts. You can give me a check and a map, and I'll get some of the boys right on the job. I think you'll find your troubles are over when my boys get there."

By the time Susannah left the office late that afternoon, she was feeling much better about the situation on the Williams Dam job site. Ed Bushnell, a retired sergeant major from the marine corps, had impressed her as being tough and capable. *If his men are anything like him,* she reflected as she started the engine of her car, *I'd certainly hate to be in the shoes of anyone caught attempting further acts of sabotage on one of Lockwood's job sites.*

Back at her condo she carried the box of Josh's papers that she'd brought with her into the house and sat it down on the kitchen table. After a light supper and a long, luxurious bath, she spent an hour going through its contents, searching for clues about Doc C or anything relating to an agreement between Josh and Adam. There was nothing, and she was angry and disgusted when the last of the scraps of paper had been consigned to the wastebasket. She couldn't help wondering if she was a fool for continuing to search so diligently for something that might not even exist.

Tuning in a radio station that specialized in music from the big band era, she turned the volume down low and tried to concentrate on a new novel she'd bought a few days ago; but Adam's face kept intruding on the pages, and she finally gave it up and turned off the lights. She spent the night tossing and turning, trying to quell the persistent, nagging hunger that prevented her from falling asleep. Adam had awakened passions in her that had been dormant for years, creating a yearning for love and closeness she'd never felt before. She bitterly regretted her carefully thought out decision to sleep with him on Friday night. It seemed that she'd been drastically mistaken about her ability to enter into a physical relationship with Adam while maintaining a degree of detachment from him on any deeper level. The powerful, thrilling, deeply satisfying ecstasy she'd experienced with him for those few hours had made it all too apparent that with her it had to be all or nothing; she either gave herself completely to a man or not at all, with no mental reservations. And, she realized with a despairing sigh, she was not prepared to unreservedly commit herself to a man about whose character there remained so many troubling questions . . .

It was long after midnight when she finally drifted into a troubled sleep.

When the alarm went off the following morning, she felt unrested and irritable. A cup of coffee and a shower did little to improve her mood, and it was only when she remembered that this was the day of her appointment with Dr. Robinson that she brightened a little. *At last,* she told herself as she got into her car to leave for the office, *I'll be learning something about the last few months of my father's life.* The thought of finding answers to some of her questions was comforting, and her mood was improved enough to appreciate the bright, sun-drenched morning as she drove toward the Lockwood yard.

Most of the morning was consumed by a meeting with Fred Ward, who was working up an estimate on another job upon which they were going to submit a bid. Fred finally left her office at eleven thirty, chortling contentedly over the figures they'd put together. He was almost certain they would be the successful bidders. Susannah was preparing to leave the office for lunch when her phone buzzed softly. When she picked up the receiver, Fran told her Adam was on the line.

"Yes, Adam?" she said, her heart quickening a little.

"Morning, boss." As always, his low baritone voice had the power to stir her. "Bill told me about the D-9. Bad, huh?"

"Yes, it is, but Bill told me that he might be able to save more of it than he thought at first."

"Yeah, that's good." He paused a moment, then changed the subject. "Those guards you sent up here look like tough bruisers. I just hope they keep their eyes open."

"They're supposed to be one of the best security agencies in the valley." She frowned slightly, wondering what he was leading up to. It was very unlike him to waste time making small talk over the telephone. "Listen, Adam," she said tentatively, "I was just getting ready to leave—"

"Okay, okay." He chuckled ruefully. "The real reason I called is to invite you to dinner at my place this Saturday night. I'm going to barbecue some steaks that'll knock your socks off, and afterward maybe we could watch a movie on my VCR . . ." When she remained silent, he quickly added, "Please say yes, Susie. Sheila's dying to meet you, and I—well, I'm sort of eager for the two of you to meet myself."

She hesitated a moment, tempted to accept but a bit wary. "I don't know, Adam. Saturday afternoon you said—"

"I said a lot of things Saturday afternoon, Susie," he interrupted. "My only excuse is that I'm in love with you, and I want you. But if the only way you'll be with me is on a—a nonphysical level, then I'll have to accept that." He paused. "I won't push you, baby. That's a promise. What do you say?"

"I say it sounds very nice, Adam," she admitted, smiling. "But I expect you to keep your word."

"I will. You can count on it. I'll pick you up around five or so, okay?"

"No," she answered firmly, "I'll drive over myself. You'll have enough to do without having to pick me up."

"Okay, then. See you Saturday."

She was feeling almost lighthearted as she gathered her things to leave for lunch. For the first time that day she felt optimistic about the future, and she was smiling as she stepped out into the bright noonday sunshine. As she got into her car and started the engine, she admitted ruefully to herself that no matter what kind of scoundrel Adam McBride might turn out to be, there was no denying that she was irretrievably in love with him. Keeping her distance was going to be increasingly difficult, when every fiber of her being ached for his caresses, for the feel of his heated skin against her flesh, and his strong, protective arms wrapped around her . . .

After a quick lunch she spent the remainder of the afternoon clearing her desk of a pile of routine paperwork, then left for her appointment with Dr. Robinson. Since noon, dark clouds had been collecting on the western horizon, and the cool breeze that stirred the leaves of the trees that lined the streets leading to the medical center smelled of rain.

She found an empty space in the small parking lot behind Dr. Robinson's office and got out of the Corvette, shivering a bit as the cool air stirred briskly. Regretting that she hadn't worn a jacket or sweater when she left home that morning, she hurried into the doctor's office.

Inside, Dr. Robinson's office was as cool and sterile as Janet's frosty voice should have led her to expect. The walls were painted a chaste white, with half a dozen poorly done oil paintings scattered around with no apparent plan. Several plastic and chrome chairs lined the walls of the small room, and on the brown carpet in the center of the room stood a glass-topped coffee table covered with old, well-thumbed issues of magazines. The wall opposite the entrance contained a glass window and counter, behind which sat a middle-aged woman eyeing Susannah expectantly through steel-rimmed spectacles. Mousy brown hair, streaked with gray, was drawn back in a severe bun, and the name plate pinned to her white blouse identified her as Janet Blackman. Suannah smiled inwardly as she approached the counter, thinking that Janet looked exactly like she sounded over the telephone.

"I'm Susannah Lockwood. I have a four-fifteen appointment."

"Oh, yes." Janet arched an eyebrow as she inspected her. "I remember you." She pursed her lips primly, then said, "We'll call you."

Taking a seat in one of the chairs, Susannah glanced around at the other occupants of the waiting room. An elderly woman sat glaring at her, and looked quickly away as Susannah nodded pleasantly. On a chair on the opposite side of the room, a young woman cradling an infant on her lap smiled tentatively but didn't speak. Susannah smiled back, then got up and took one of the magazines.

Finally, just before five o'clock, Janet called her, opening the door to one side of the counter. Susannah walked through the door, then followed Janet down a gleaming tiled hallway to an empty examination room. The room contained a table, a chair, and a sink with foot pedals to operate the water taps.

"Doctor will be right with you," Janet said, holding the door open and indicating that Susannah should enter. Susannah sat down on the chair in the tiny room and waited another fifteen minutes, this time without the benefit of even a magazine to distract her. The minutes crawled by. It was almost exactly an hour past the time of her appointment when the door opened and a middle-aged, harried-looking man with thinning red hair walked briskly into the room. In his hand was a manila folder. When he opened the folder, he frowned at the sight of the blank medical chart within.

"Miss Lockwood . . ." He looked at her with puzzlement in his gray eyes. "What seems to be the problem today? Janet neglected to open a chart on you," he added, the puzzlement in his eyes giving way to irritation.

"Dr. Robinson," Susannah said as he started to open the door, "I'm not here for a medical problem. All I want is to ask you a few questions about my father, Joshua Lockwood. He was a regular patient of yours, I understand."

"You want to talk about your father?" Dr. Robinson frowned at her, his blunt fingers nervously tapping the blank chart in the folder. He shook his head. "Miss Lockwood, surely you must realize that my patients are entitled to privacy? Communication between a patient and his physician is—"

"My father is dead, Dr. Robinson," Susannah interrupted. "I have reason to suspect," she hesitated, then, blurted, "that he might have committed suicide."

"I see," Dr. Robinson murmured, after studying her narrowly for a moment. "And you suspect that something in his medical history may shed some light on his reasons?"

"Yes, I do."

"In that case . . ." Dr. Robinson turned and opened the door of the treatment room, peering down the short hallway. "Janet," he called, "bring me our chart on Mr. Lockwood, please. First name"—he glanced back at Susannah, who quickly supplied the information—"Joshua."

As he turned back from the open doorway, he studied Susannah for a few seconds, then asked, "What exactly were the circumstances of your father's death, Miss Lockwood, that lead you to suspect he might have killed himself?"

Briefly she told him what she had learned about her father's fatal accident. When she finished, Dr. Robinson grunted noncommittally, accepting the thick medical chart that Janet thrust into his hand. Closing the door behind him, he quickly leafed through the chart, flipping the pages, shaking his head occasionally, and muttering as he finished the last page and closed the chart.

"The last time I saw your father was last May, Miss Lockwood. And that was just for a routine physical." He scratched his head, frowning in thought. "I remember him now, I think. Big fellow, with dark curly hair? Right. Strange . . ."

"What?" Susannah asked, leaning forward expectantly, as the doctor's voice trailed off into silence. "What was strange?"

"Well, his physical turned up nothing unusual." He glanced up sharply. "You knew he was a borderline diabetic, of course?" Susannah nodded, and he went on, "Other than watching his diet very closely and keeping his weight down, he didn't have any problems to speak of. Heart, lungs, both okay. Blood pressure was right in the ballpark for a man his age . . ."

"So what's strange about all that?" Susannah pressed, a trace of impatience in her voice.

"It wasn't the physical itself, Miss Lockwood," the doctor said, shaking his head slowly. "What I seem to recall is that he mentioned a pain in his armpits—well, not a pain, so much," he corrected himself, flipping the folder open again and studying the final entry on the chart, "more of an irritation." He frowned, closing the chart. "I told him to schedule another appointment and we'd check it out for him, but he never came back in."

"Did he happen to ask what could possibly cause such an irritation in his armpits?"

"Yes, he did, and that's what's strange about the fact he never scheduled another appointment." The doctor paused, rubbing the bridge of his nose between thumb and forefinger, sighing wearily. "I told him that the most *common* reason for such an irritation would be clogged pores, leading to an irritation in his glands." Removing his hand, he looked at her with raised eyebrows. "But I also warned him that an irritation like that *could* be an early symptom of certain types of cancer."

The forbidding word echoed grimly in her mind as she left the doctor's office and hurried through the stiff, cold breeze toward her car. Fat drops of rain began smacking against the fiberglass roof of the Corvette as she sat there for a moment, deep in thought. *Could fear of cancer alone have been the reason for Dad's final, desperate action?* she wondered. Josh had been such a baby about doctors and illnesses, she remembered, and had dreaded the infirmities of old age with a horror wildly out of proportion with any possible reality.

When Josh had been diagnosed as mildly diabetic, she recalled as she started the engine and backed out of the parking slot, he'd taken to his bed for an entire weekend, driving her and Julia to distraction with his fretting over the possibility of having to inject himself with insulin on a daily basis for the rest of his life. He'd been pathetically, almost comically, relieved when his doctor informed him that his diabetes could be controlled by strict attention to his diet.

Indeed, this was one of the reasons Susannah was so certain that Josh hadn't been drinking the night he drove his car over that cliff in the San Gabriel Canyon. He hadn't touched alcohol in any form since learning of his diabetes, and he'd been fanatical about keeping to his strict diet in order to control the disease without insulin. So whatever his state of mind had been on that fateful night, she would have been willing to bet that his judgment hadn't been affected by alcohol.

What was appalling to her was the possibility that Joshua, a man she had always idolized, could have been such a coward, taking the quick and easy way out of a dreadful predicament. *Of course, I have no proof of this,* she reminded herself, shifting gears automatically as she pulled away from a traffic signal. She reached out and switched on the windshield wipers; the rain was coming down steadily now and looked as if it would continue on through the night.

Knowing Josh as she did, she had to admit that suicide would hold more appeal to him than spending the last several months or years of his life as a cancer patient, slowly wasting away, as doctors tried to prolong a life that had lost all its savor, all its sweetness. That by doing so he had inflicted an unshakable burden of guilt upon his wife, and had deprived his only child of any opportunity to spend time with her father, indicated a thoughtlessness, a selfishness, that created a deep feeling of anger and resentment in Susannah.

By the time she turned off the main street into her neighborhood, the conviction that that was indeed what had happened—that her adored father had chosen the easy way out in order to avoid a long, painful battle with a vicious disease—had taken firm root in her mind.

And yet, she reflected as she parked in the carport and hurried into the house, she still had no proof that this was what had happened, and *proof* was what she wanted to be able to present to Julia. She put on a stack of Glenn Miller records, realizing as the familiar music filled the air that finding the elusive Doc C had taken on new urgency, now that she felt so strongly she was on the trail of the truth. And for her own peace of mind, as well as Julia's, discovering the truth was more vital than ever.

CHAPTER EIGHT

Adam couldn't have picked a nicer day for a barbecue, Susannah thought as she drove down a broad, shady street with the sunroof of her Corvette cranked open, the mild breeze created by the motion of the car playing pleasantly with her hair and skin. At five o'clock the sun was low in the sky, but the temperature remained in the mideighties. The evening promised to be mild and balmy, and she had dressed for the occasion in a light, silky white jumpsuit cinched around the waist with a broad red leather belt. She wore matching red sandals on her feet, and a red scarf was knotted loosely around her throat.

As she stopped at an intersection, she glanced down at the hand-drawn map Adam had dropped off at her office Friday morning. He lived on the next street, at the end of a cul-de-sac. Susannah pulled away from the intersection and flicked on her turn signal, preparing to turn onto his street. She studied the pleasant neighborhood as she drove, noticing the broad driveways, manicured lawns, and shrubbery. Adam had come up in the world since the days he and his wife lived in a mobile home.

She pulled over to the curb in front of Adam's house and sat in the car for a moment, looking it over. Adam's lot occupied a pie-shaped piece of land at the very apex of the cul-de-sac. The home appealed to her at first glance: it was a beige, two-story house with chocolate-brown trim on the windows, doors, and eaves and a brown tiled mansard roof. At one end of the house, a brick chimney indicated the presence of a fireplace. *Yes,* she decided, *it's a very nice home.* As she got out of her car, she noticed that the lush green lawn had recently been mowed and edged.

She walked up the driveway, past Adam's big pickup, and took the sidewalk that led to the front door. She rang the bell. Immediately, as if she'd been watching through the front window for Susannah's arrival, a small girl wearing a frilly, light blue and white dress with puffy sleeves and white shoes looked through the screen door. Susannah recognized the blond, curly-haired child as Adam's daughter from the photograph he'd shown her, but the photo hadn't prepared her for the strength and intelligence that fairly radiated from the little girl's bright blue eyes.

"Are you Susannah?" she asked with frank curiosity.

"Yes, I am." Susannah smiled down at her. "And you're Sheila. I recognize you from your pictures, but you're much prettier in person."

"Thank you," the child said gravely. "Come on in. My father is in the bathroom right now, but he'll be out in a minute."

Susannah opened the screen door, and Sheila led her into a spacious living room. Looked around approvingly, Susannah took a seat on the large, leather-covered sofa. It was a man's room, she observed, but it was one in which a woman could be very comfortable. The walls were covered with dark, glossy, walnut paneling and hung with several paintings, mostly seascapes, but with a few western landscapes included, apparently for variety. There were several framed photographs as well, most of them of construction sites she assumed Adam must have worked on at one time or another, along with a few portraits of people who were probably members of his family.

Most of the furniture seemed somewhat oversized to her and was covered by leather or tweed in rich earth tones. Cream-colored drapes at the windows relieved the somber paneled walls, and the thick orange and brown shag carpet somehow pulled all the disparate elements of the room into a unified whole. With the various styles of furniture and the seemingly unplanned decorating scheme, it shouldn't have worked, but somehow it did. Instead of feeling somber and grim, the room radiated an ambience of warmth and hospitality. She leaned back on the sofa and relaxed, smiling at the little girl who was watching her soberly with enormous blue eyes.

"Would you like something to drink?" Sheila asked.

"Maybe when your father joins us," Susannah replied, forcibly reminding herself that this child was not yet four years old.

"Hi!" Adam came into the room, his teeth flashing against his darkly tanned face. Leaning over, he gave her a kiss on the cheek, and she breathed in the aromas of soap and shaving lotion. "You look like a million bucks! I see you two ladies have met, so I don't need to do the honors. Ready for a drink?"

"Well, maybe a glass of iced tea, if you have it." She watched him as he turned to leave the room. He was dressed in a pair of pale-blue slacks and white canvas deck shoes, along with a white knit shirt that was dazzling against the bronze of his throat and arms. "Is there something I can help you with?" she called after him.

"You just sit there and get to know Sheila," he responded from the kitchen. In a moment he returned, carrying a tray on which sat three drinks—a tall tumbler of iced tea for her, a small glass of orange juice for Sheila, and a can of beer for himself. When everyone was served, he sat down in a chair directly across from Susannah and smiled again. "I'm sure glad you came," he said softly, his eyes glowing with happiness. "Would you like to see the rest of the house?"

"Maybe later." She lowered her eyes, feeling the revealing heat in her face. Sheila was seated a few inches away from her on the sofa, studying her with a composure that was unusual in a child of her age. "Sheila, you're a very pretty little girl."

"I'm a *big* girl," Sheila corrected her. "Daddy always says so."

"Of course you are." Susannah glanced over at Adam, who shrugged as if to say that Sheila had a mind of her own.

"Are you going to eat with us?" Sheila asked.

"Do you want me to?"

"Yes." The child hopped down from the sofa and stood in front of Susannah. "Would you like to see my room?"

"Very much," Susannah replied, flattered by the child's obviously sincere invitation. She looked over at Adam and raised her eyebrows inquiringly.

"I've got to check the coals," he said, waving them away. "You two go ahead. I'll join you in a few minutes."

The child gravely took her hand, leading her toward the flight of stairs that led to the second story. Framed photographs hung along the wall next to the stairs, and Susannah looked at each of them as they climbed, trying to guess their identities.

"That's my mother." Sheila was proudly pointing at a framed portrait near the top of the stairs. Susannah studied the lovely young face in the photograph curiously. The brown-haired young woman had been smiling at the camera, her dark-blue eyes sparkling with zest for life.

"She's very pretty," Susannah murmured.

"She's dead," Sheila stated in a matter-of-fact tone. "She burned up in a fire when I was just a baby." She gave Susannah's hand an impatient tug. "C'mon, this is my room. That's Daddy's room, down the hall." She opened the door of her room and stood aside, watching Susannah's face for her reaction.

"It's very nice, Sheila." Susannah studied the interior of the room thoughtfully. Something wasn't right, but she couldn't put her finger on it right away. The room was lovely, decorated in pink and white, with a lacy bedspread on the canopied bed. An array of dolls were carefully displayed on the shelves against the walls, their tiny dresses spread to display themselves to best advantage. *They're like illustrations in a catalog*, Susannah reflected.

"It's—you keep it very neat," she said faintly. Then it struck her: the room was entirely *too* neat; it was more like the room of an extremely fussy twelve-year-old than that of a three-year-old.

"Yes, I do," Sheila agreed. "It helps Mrs. Lopez. She's the lady who stays with me while Daddy works. She's nice, but she likes to keep everything neat." She walked over to the other side of her bed, gesturing to Susannah with childlike animation as she said, "Look at my dollhouse."

As she stepped around the end of the bed, Susannah stopped, gasping in admiration. The dollhouse was a miniature replica of the house in which they were standing, constructed with incredible attention to detail, right down to the cream-colored drapes hanging in the downstairs windows and a tiny brass doorknob on the front door. Sheila knelt and touched a concealed switch, and the tiny windows lit up, adding to the illusion of reality.

"This is just beautiful!" Susannah knelt and reached tentatively for the tiny front door. The door opened smoothly, and she leaned down and peered inside. The rooms were filled with miniature furniture, and tiny framed pictures hung on the paneled walls. "This is really incredible," she murmured, looking over her shoulder at Sheila. "Where ever did you find this?"

"My Daddy made it for me," Sheila boasted, smiling broadly for the first time since Susannah's arrival, revealing something of the child locked inside the tiny adult.

"Adam?" Susannah turned back to the dollhouse, narrowing her eyes in concentration. "Your daddy *built* this?"

"Um-hum." Sheila's eyes glowed with pride. "You should see his trains. They're down in the garage."

"I'll show them to you later, if you're really interested." Adam stood in the doorway of Sheila's room, smiling at the two of them with a proprietary expression in his eyes. Flustered, Susannah quickly got to her feet, brushing off the knees of her jumpsuit. "Right now," he continued, "the steaks are ready to go on the fire. How do you want yours cooked?"

"Charred on the outside, pink on the inside." Susannah gestured toward the intricately constructed dollhouse, over her embarrassment at having been caught on her knees like a child. "Adam, this is exquisite. I had no idea you could do things like this."

"I told you I was interested in model railroading," he said, shrugging modestly. "This is just a sideline." Putting his arm around her shoulder, he took his daughter by the hand. "Come on, ladies, let's go cook some steaks."

As they descended the stairs and turned to the left, away from the living room, Susannah noticed that his kitchen was similar to Julia's—there was a large dining area adjacent to the kitchen, and a sliding glass door led out onto the patio. They passed through the open door onto the patio, where a portable barbecue stood next to a folding table on which there was a platter of thick red steaks. On the other side of the patio was a redwood picnic table, set with paper plates and flatware. The vast backyard was covered with grass that had not been as recently mowed as the front, and a couple of orange trees near the back fence were covered with snowy blossoms.

"Is there anything I can do to help?" she asked as Adam put the steaks on the grill. With a searing noise the delicious aroma of cooking beef permeated the air, filling her with anticipation. She hadn't realized she was so hungry. "Make a salad, maybe?"

"Everything's under control, Susie." His smile caused her heart to skip a beat, and she felt a surge of self-disgust at the emotions she didn't seem able to control. She was like a high-school girl around Adam, a high-school girl on her first date with the football hero on whom she had a terrific crush. "When I invite guests," Adam continued in a jocular tone, "I don't expect them to have to do any of the work. Tell you what, though," he grinned, "you could get me a fresh beer."

"Coming right up, chef," she said, grateful for the opportunity to do something besides make a fool of herself.

"I'll show you where the refrigerator is," Sheila offered, coming over and taking Susannah's hand in her much smaller one.

"Grab a beer for yourself, if you're ready," Adam called after them. "Or if you'd rather have more iced tea, it's in the refrigerator, too."

"Daddy likes beer," Sheila stated matter-of-factly as they entered the kitchen. "He always keeps some in the refrigerator."

"Along with some soda for you?" Susannah asked teasingly, smiling at the diminutive little person at her side.

"No, I don't like soda very much," Sheila replied, opening the door of the refrigerator with a grunt of effort. "There's the beer, and the iced tea's in that big fat pitcher."

"Thanks." Susannah smiled wryly as she extracted two cans from the shelf, wondering briefly if she should offer one to Sheila. "You're very grown up for your age, Sheila."

"Of course. I *am* the woman of the house, you know." Sheila shot Susannah a sidelong glance as she pushed the refrigerator door closed. "That's what Daddy always tells me, anyway."

"I see." She followed the child back out onto the patio, a bit nonplussed by her continuing adultlike behavior. It required a conscious effort to remember that Sheila was, after all, not quite four years old.

Adam glanced over as they reappeared and raised his eyebrows questioningly at the expression on Susannah's face. She just smiled slightly and shook her head. He looked at Sheila, back at Susannah, and nodded in understanding. As he accepted the can of cold beer, he leaned over and kissed her on the cheek. "She's quite a kid, isn't she?" he whispered proudly.

She glanced around and saw that the child was busily checking the arrangement of paper plates on the picnic table. "She certainly is," she replied ruefully. "It's almost scary, she's so mature for her age."

"*Too* mature, really." A troubled expression crossed his face, then he shook his head and smiled broadly. "Steaks are ready. Is anybody hungry?"

"I'm famished!" Susannah inhaled the aroma that wafted up from the grill as he lifted the steaks onto a waiting platter.

"Sit down, Susie. I'll get the rest of the food." He entered the house, returning after a moment with a large bowl of salad and three baked potatoes on a platter. After placing a steaming potato on each of their plates, he ladled some salad onto his daughter's plate.

Susannah glanced around the table while she split her potato and dropped a chunk of butter into the piping hot interior. She smiled when she noticed that Sheila had neglected to put napkins on the table but said nothing. It was almost reassuring to discover this childish lapse, she realized with a twinge of amusement. Adam must have noticed as well, because he hurried back into the kitchen, returning after a moment with a handful of paper napkins, which he passed around before cutting into his steak.

"This is delicious!" Susannah exclaimed after swallowing the first bite of her steak. "I'm surprised that you cook so well."

"Had to learn," he replied easily, slicing off a bite of meat. "After Sheila and I were on our own, I had to learn a lot of things: cook, clean house, change diapers. Nowadays it's not so bad, since we have Mrs. Lopez, but the first year or so I had a good taste of what it's like to be a wife and mother." He put the meat in his mouth and chewed rapidly, shaking his head. "Anybody who thinks *that's* not a job," he said after swallowing, "is a fool."

When they finished eating, Susannah insisted on

cleaning up while Adam went into the living room and loaded a video cassette for Sheila to watch before going to bed. There was surprisingly little to do, and she was finished in a couple of minutes.

"I picked up Snow White at the video store for you to watch tonight, honey," Adam said when he came back into the kitchen. "Are you ready? I'd like to show Susannah my trains, if she's really interested."

"I most certainly am interested," Susannah declared.

"Snow White!" Sheila exclaimed happily. "I'm ready."

They followed Adam into the living room, where Sheila scooted up onto the sofa, her hands folded primly in her lap, watching expectantly while Adam pushed the play button on the VCR unit. In a moment the screen was filled with the animated images of the old Disney movie, and Sheila's lips curved in an oddly solemn little smile.

"Ready?" Adam smiled at Susannah as he took her hand and led her toward the door in the kitchen that led into the garage. Her skin tingled at the contact, but she made no move to pull away.

"I've converted most of the garage into a regular machine shop," he explained as he flicked on the light switch just inside the door. Fluorescent lighting flickered, then glowed steadily, brightly illuminating the interior of the large garage. Susannah's eyes glowed in admiration as she stood taking in the scene.

Lathes, drills, saws, shapers, cutting torches, and other esoteric machines at whose function she could only guess occupied over half the floor space. Running down one wall, the one on the kitchen side of the garage, was a sturdy workbench, equipped with vises and clamps. On the wall behind the workbench dozens of hand tools hung on individually marked pegs.

The remainder of the garage was taken up by a miniature railroad, which ran in a series of loops through an amazingly detailed little town. Leaving the town, the rails ran through a few yards of countryside, then climbed into a mountainous area, complete with a three-foot-long tunnel. Several trains sat on sidings, some made up of passenger cars, others of freight cars of all descriptions. She stood transfixed with delight as Adam touched a switch and one of the trains began to move forward, the large driver arms on the side of the engine laboring realistically.

"Adam, it's—it's fabulous!"

"Thanks. The setup represents the early thirties," he explained, smiling proudly. "From about the Civil War up until the midthirties, that was the heyday of steam locomotives. In the forties everything started gradually converting to diesel." He paused, smiling at her. "But I don't think the diesels have the magic of the old steam locomotives."

She shook her head in agreement. "They're just exquisite, Adam." She bent closer, examining the tiny cross ties and steel rails upon which the little train was traveling. "I always thought toy trains were for—"

"Little kids?" he interrupted, shaking his head. "Sure, kids like train sets. Electric trains will always be popular with some, I suppose. But this kind of hobby"—he gestured expressively at the intricate layout—"is pretty much for grown men, Susie. Take that engine there. I've got nearly two hundred hours of labor in it."

"You *built* that engine?" she asked in amazement.

"Most of it. Some of the parts I picked up ready-made, but the bulk of it I turned out right here in the garage." He touched the switch, and the small train backed onto its siding next to the others. "This is an HO gauge set up here, so I bought the running gears ready-made and built the rest of the locomotives around them." He beckoned for her to follow, walking toward what had once been the big overhead garage door, where something bulky, covered by a sheet of canvas, rested on a pair of saw horses.

"Now this," he said, whipping off the canvas with a flourish, "is really going to be something. This is a *live* steam engine, Susie. Two-and-a-half-inch scale, built to run on a seven-and-a-half-inch track. This baby'll have enough power to pull several hundred pounds of cargo when it's finished."

"Adam . . . this is just amazing." She stepped nearer, putting out her hand to touch the boiler of the immaculately detailed locomotive. The engine was about two feet long and looked to her as if it could blow its steam whistle and go puffing away at a moment's notice. "Live steam, you said?"

"That's right," he confirmed. "This engine is going to be a completely scaled version of a 1900 Baldwin locomotive." He paused, running a hand over the dull black finish on the roof of the engineer's cab. "I've probably got less than a hundred hours' work left on this baby. But then I've got to make a tender to go with it, of course . . ." He looked up at her as he went on, "There's a club up in Montecito where live-steam fanatics bring their trains once a year for a three-day meet. Guys come from all over the country to run their engines over more than a mile of track." Smiling, he lovingly replaced the canvas cover on the replica. "I'd like to be there when they have their next meet." As he turned to face her, his smile slowly faded and his eyes filled with desire. She was helpless to resist as he drew her slowly into the strong circle of his arms.

"I'd like you and Sheila to be with me when that day comes," he said huskily, the timbre of his voice sending shivers down her spine.

"Adam, I . . ."

Her voice faded as his firm, warm lips came down and covered her mouth. She felt her knees turning to water and placed her arms around his neck for support, moaning as she felt his warm tongue probing gently at her lips. She felt her lips open slightly to permit the entry of his tongue, amazed at her inability to resist. As his tongue seared her lips and the inside of her mouth, intense waves of pleasure radiated through her body, making her tremble with need. His big, strong hands were exploring her, pulling her against him, and a delicious feeling of lassitude began creeping over her, destroying any will she had to resist. *I've got to stop this,* she thought. But at the same time, she felt her body's betrayal, as her pelvis pushed against his lean, masculine hardness, sending wave after wave of desire radiating out from her fiery core, carrying her relentlessly toward what promised to be a shattering crescendo of ecstasy.

"Adam, no!" she moaned, twisting her mouth away from his, surprised at how faint her voice sounded to her own ears. "I . . . I can't, Adam."

"Yes, you can!" He groaned hoarsely, twisting her head back around to meet his lips with a power she knew she couldn't resist much longer. His other hand was gently rubbing the lower part of her abdomen, creating a heat that threatened to explode into a flame that could be extinguished in only one way.

"Oh, please, Adam," she said, twisting away with her last remaining vestige of resistance. "What about Sheila?"

His grip suddenly weakened, and she escaped his arms, sagging against the end of the workbench for support. She wiped the back of her mouth with a trembling hand, feeling the turbulent emotions gradually subsiding as she watched sanity slowly returning to his face.

"That's right," he breathed, a bewildered expression on his face. "Sheila's still up." The stunned expression left his eyes, and he grinned ruefully at her, staring hungrily at her. Gradually his eyes lost the glazed, unfocused look, returning to their normal expression of slightly amused detachment. "Wow," he muttered, running a hand through his thick, blond hair, "that started out to be just a friendly little kiss, Susie. Whew!" He looked up at her, smiling apologetically, shaking his head. "I guess it's kind of hard to give just a friendly little kiss when you're as crazy about the one you're kissing as I am."

"It's—it's not easy for me, either," she replied, passing a hand over her eyes again. She felt a little calmer when she looked up at him again. "Adam, I realize my attitude must seem crazy to you, but please try to understand."

"I'll give it a hell of a try, Susie, but you're going to have to help me if it's going to work." He swallowed, the smooth bronze muscles of his throat working visibly, and his eyes continued to devour her. "I just don't think I could control myself if we kissed like that again."

"We just won't, that's all," she said stoutly, feeling a growing warmth toward him for his willingness to honor her wishes, no matter how strange they must seem to him. A tiny part of the niggling doubt about his character seemed to shrivel and die as she looked at him. She sighed inwardly. *If only I could find that damned elusive paper he claims to have signed*, she thought exasperatedly, *the last of my doubts would be resolved and I could put an end to this agony.*

She felt relaxed enough to take his hand as they started out of the garage; and when he gave hers a little squeeze, she returned the pressure. It was reassuring to her in a way she didn't begin to understand.

They entered the living room just in time to see the credits rolling across the television screen. Sheila climbed down from the sofa, yawning and smiling, looking more like a normal three-year-old child than she had at any time since Susannah's arrival.

"That was good, Daddy."

"I thought you'd like it. Now, it's bedtime for you, sweetheart." He leaned down to scoop her up into his arms, but she twisted away, scowling.

"I can walk," she protested.

"Guess this just ain't my day," he observed with a rueful glance at Susannah. "How about a good-night kiss?" he asked his daughter. "And don't tell me you're too big for that."

She smiled as she put her small arms around his neck and kissed him on the lips. When he released her, she stepped back and looked up at Susannah. "Good night."

"Good night, Sheila," Susannah said warmly. "It was a pleasure meeting you, and I hope to see you again."

Sheila nodded and turned toward the staircase. As she put her foot on the bottom riser, she glanced back at Susannah and smiled. "I hope to see you again, too."

"How about pouring us each a glass of wine?" Adam smiled at her from the foot of the staircase. "I'll go up and tuck her in, then maybe we can talk awhile. Okay?"

"I don't know, Adam," she replied doubtfully, glancing at her watch. "I really should get going . . ."

"Oh, come on," he said, winking, "you can stay a little longer. You did plan to spend the evening, didn't you?" When she didn't reply, he touched her cheek, smiled, then hurried up the stairs after his daughter.

Although she knew she should be leaving, Susannah went into the kitchen and found a bottle of chilled white wine in the refrigerator. As she poured it into two glasses and carried them into the living room, she found herself thinking how pleasant it would be if she didn't have to go home at all, if she could just stay . . .

"All tucked in for the night," Adam announced as he came down the stairs. He sat down beside her on the sofa and clicked his wine glass against hers. "Here's to the future—together, I hope."

"The future," she murmured, smiling.

"So, what do you think of my daughter?" he asked, replacing the wine glass on the coffee table and leaning back on the sofa.

"She's quite a kid." Susannah hesitated for a moment, frowning slightly. "She's so—so darned mature for her age that it's almost weird. Hasn't she ever been just a little girl?"

"Not really." He linked his hands behind his head, looking serious but relaxed. "It's been pretty rough on her, growing up without Ann . . . You know, she's so damned *strong*. Sheila has a kind of inner strength that I find myself relying on, depending on, almost as if she were the parent and I was the child." He chuckled, shaking his head in puzzlement. "I look at her and I see her mother's eyes looking back at me"—he fell silent for a moment, and when he looked up at her his eyes were filled with guilt—"almost as if they were accusing me."

"Oh, Adam, how could that be?" she said sympathetically, laying her hand against his cheek and looking into his eyes. "You must be imagining it."

"Maybe." He put his hand over hers, then moved his lips across her palm. "But it seems very real at the time."

"Do you think she likes me?" Susannah asked, changing the subject, wanting to get away from his feelings of guilt. There was something deep down inside that was troubling him, she knew, remembering the vehement way he'd denied any culpability in the fire that killed his wife.

"Oh, I know she does," he assured her, laughing softly, the troubled expression leaving his eyes. "She's never asked anyone to come back again—until you."

And we won't go into the implications of that, Susannah thought. However, she couldn't help wondering just how many women had been invited here for dinner and inspection by Adam's daughter. Instead, she mentioned Julia's dancing lessons and asked if he thought Sheila might enjoy them.

"Hey, she might like that," he replied enthusiastically. "And it'd probably be the best thing in the world to help get her out of that little old lady shell of hers." He paused, then added, "Next to having you around on a full-time basis, that is."

The remark hung in the air between them for a moment, then she took his hand. His fingers curled around hers with tender strength.

"I don't suppose you've changed your mind"—she whispered softly—"about marriage?"

He lifted her hand to his lips and nuzzled it lovingly, shaking his head regretfully. "There's nothing I'd like more than to be married to you, Susie. But you know how I feel about marrying my way into the company."

"Oh, Adam," she murmured, her voice breaking just a little, "sometimes I think it's going to drive me right out of my mind. Why are you so damned stubborn and proud?"

"You wouldn't love me if I wasn't," he said hoarsely, laying a finger against her lips as she opened her mouth to protest. "Truce, okay? For tonight, let's just be two people who are very much in love, without anything lying around to complicate matters."

"Just forget about the whole darned world, you mean?" she whispered, staring into his eyes, loving him for the suggestion. "Job . . . family . . . friends?"

"Everything but you and me," he repeated huskily, staring at her, his light-blue eyes glowing with hunger. "Is it a deal, Susie?"

"Oh, yes, my love," she whispered, melting into his arms as he drew her close. "For tonight, it's a deal."

As he scooped her into his arms and began walking up the stairs with her, she laid her head against his chest, reveling in the easy strength with which he carried her, surrendering, just for tonight, to the love she couldn't help feeling for him. *Just for tonight,* she thought as he gently laid her down on the big double bed in his room, *just for tonight . . .*

Later, she opened her eyes and peered drowsily at the illuminated dial of his alarm clock. Three A.M. She sighed, stretching langorously, her entire body seeming to glow with the aftermath of their lovemaking, and swung her legs over the side of the bed.

"Baby?" Adam muttered, putting his hand on her leg in the dark. "What're you doing?"

"I've got to go home," she whispered. "We can't have Sheila walking in and finding us like this in the morning."

He switched on one of the bedside lamps and sat up in bed, running his hands through his short, crisp blond hair. "At this hour? Be sensible. Lay back down and get some sleep."

"Adam, we can't," she protested softly. "I'd like to stay, but what kind of example would we be setting for Sheila?"

"Well, it just seems crazy, that's all." He got out of bed and slipped into a velour robe, staring at her. "I don't see why you have to go running off in the middle of the night this way."

"Adam, please don't be this way. I want to have Sheila's respect, if we're to have a good relationship." She slipped into her shoes and walked over to him, patting him fondly on the cheek. "If we were married—"

"We've been through all that," he replied sharply. "You know how I feel. I'm not going to be anybody's poor relative, not even yours, no matter how much I love you."

She stared at him, tears of anger filling her eyes. "I see," she said bitterly. "You don't mind sleeping with me at your convenience, but you're just too proud to marry me as long as I own the company that employs you. Forgive me if I'm wrong, but there seems to be a strange sort of double standard in effect here, Adam, and it puzzles the hell out of me. You claim to be in love with me, but marriage is out of the question unless I can come up with that imaginary piece of paper you say—"

"Just a damned minute," he snapped. "There's nothing *imaginary* about that paper Josh signed. But you've never believed me, have you? All along, you seemed to have thought I was trying some sort of scam to defraud you out of part of your precious company!"

"Adam, please," she remonstrated, glancing anxiously at the door. "Lower your voice. You'll wake Sheila!"

"Dammit, I—" Abruptly he sagged, sitting back down on the bed. Softly he said, "I don't lie, Susannah. Josh made that agreement with me, and that's a fact. Just because you can't find his copy doesn't mean it never existed."

She sat down next to him, leaning her head against his bare shoulder, wishing she didn't have to go. "The last few months of Dad's life, he was very troubled. He . . ."

"He what?"

"Nothing." At the last moment she changed her mind

about telling him what she suspected of her father's death. "He just wasn't himself, that's all."

"You sure as hell don't have to tell me that," he snorted. "I'm the guy who kept the company above water—until you came back. I went for days without even *seeing* Josh, Susie. Once I even had to forge his name on the payroll checks." He shook his head wearily. "No, you don't have to tell me he wasn't himself," he repeated.

"He had problems," she murmured.

"Problems?" She felt him stiffen, and she moved her head off his shoulder. "I don't much care *what* Josh's problems were, Susie. All I know is that his negligence is creating one hell of a rift between you and me, just when everything could be so right between us."

"His negligence?" she flared angrily, in spite of her resolve not to fight with him tonight. "What about your own? I haven't seen your copy of the famous agreement either!"

His face was white when he turned to face her, his lips drawn back over his teeth in a grimace of anger. "Dammit, I've told you before, that fire was *not* any fault of mine!"

"Oh, really? Well, I find it a little strange that you have to deny it so vehemently," she said, hating herself the moment the words left her mouth. "Oh, Adam I didn't mean that! I'm so sor—"

"I think you'd better leave now," he muttered hoarsely, looking down at the floor.

"Adam, please—"

"Go!"

Stifling a sob, Susannah rose to leave the room. At that instant the phone shrilled harshly, startling both of them. Adam stared incredulously at his alarm clock, then snatched up the receiver. "McBride," he snapped.

After listening for several seconds he exclaimed, "What? How the hell could that happen? What about the guards?"

Susannah paused in the doorway, glancing back inquiringly. Adam stared blankly at her as he listened, signaling for her to wait.

"Okay, I'll come up at sunup," he said, then replaced the receiver.

"What happened?"

"Another case of sabotage on the job." He cinched the belt of his robe and got to his feet. When he faced her again, the old mocking glint was back in his eyes; the mockery, she realized now, was his way of hiding the pain and guilt he lived with. "Guess the guards aren't as good as they're cracked up to be, huh?"

CHAPTER NINE

The crackling roar of an inconsiderate neighbor's motorcycle woke Susannah early on Sunday morning. Before she could roll over and go back to sleep, the memory of last night's ugly quarrel with Adam flooded back into her mind. When she remembered the phone call informing them of another case of suspected sabotage on the canyon job, she groaned and opened her eyes, peering blearily at the digital display of her bedside alarm clock. It was just after seven. She laid there for a few more minutes, then sat up, feeling groggy and unrested.

She spent an hour reading the Sunday paper and drinking coffee, then picked up the phone and dialed Julia's number.

"I don't know if I feel up to keeping our breakfast date this morning," she said when her stepmother came on the line. She told Julia about the problem on the job site, finishing up by saying, "So I need to drive up there and find out firsthand what happened."

Julia was silent for a moment, then suggested, "Why don't I go with you? I've never been up in the canyon, and if you wouldn't mind the company, maybe we could make it a lunch date instead?"

Susannah thought for a moment. Under different circumstances she would have been riding up to the canyon with Adam. Still, she had no desire to spend the morning alone, moping over problems she seemed powerless to solve, adding to the depression she was unable to shake off. Perhaps Julia's company would cheer her up.

"Why not?" she replied. "We can look things over up there, then have lunch on our way back."

The sun was glaring down from a cloudless sky by the time she stopped in front of Julia's house and tapped the horn. Although it was not yet ten o'clock, the temperature was climbing steadily through the eighties and would reach the mid nineties before the day was over, according to the weather forecast she'd just heard on the car radio. It was still early May, but an unseasonable heat wave had descended over southern California, aggravated by the hot, dry Santa Ana winds that accompanied it.

"Good morning," Julia greeted brightly as she hurried down the sidewalk and got into the car. Like Susannah, she was dressed for the weather in a pair of walking shorts and a light, sleeveless top. She looked at Susannah's face for a moment and shook her head. "Uh-oh. Dark circles under the eyes, kid. Another fight with Adam?"

"He's such a pigheaded fool sometimes," she said, putting the car in gear and pulling away from the curb. "If I wasn't so crazy about him, my life would be a lot simpler!"

"But probably duller," Julia chimed in with a grin. "What is it you two keep going on about? Does he find it hard to work for a woman?"

"No, it's not that." Susannah sighed as she stopped at a traffic signal, checked oncoming traffic, then turned right on Foothill Boulevard, heading toward Azusa. The traffic was light, and when she had shifted into high gear, she glanced over and smiled ruefully.

"We get along just fine, as far as the job is concerned. Adam respects me as an engineer . . . It's just—oh, I don't know, Julia. I probably shouldn't burden you with my troubles."

"If not me, then who?" Julia demanded with asperity. "I'm the only mother you've got, and I thought I was your friend as well. If you can't confide in me, I'm pretty much a failure in both departments, aren't I?"

"No, you're terrific in both departments." Susannah thought for several moments, oddly reluctant to tell her stepmother anything that might lower her opinion of Adam. And yet, she realized, if she couldn't unburden herself to someone, and soon, she was afraid she might just burst.

"It might help, honey," Julia soothed, reaching over to pat her hand. Her kind tone of voice was Susannah's undoing, and she felt the quick hot sting of tears behind her eyelids as the urge to open up suddenly became unbearable.

"Adam's got this—this obsession," she blurted. "He told me back in January that Dad made an agreement to sign over a quarter of the company to him on his tenth anniversary with the company." She shifted down into third gear, slowing for the ramp onto the 210 freeway, which would take them to Azusa, the small city at the base of the San Gabriel Canyon. She didn't speak again until the Corvette was in high gear, speeding down the freeway at sixty miles an hour.

"His tenth anniversary with the company was in March."

Julia nodded thoughtfully, turning in the seat to face Susannah more directly. "How is that a problem, Susie? If they had an agreement—"

"The problem is that Adam's copy of the agreement" —her lips twisted sourly—"*if* it ever existed, burned up in the fire when he lost his home."

"And his wife," Julia murmured.

"Yes, of course." Susannah glanced over at Julia. "And I can't find the copy Dad supposedly kept in any of his stuff."

Julia nodded slowly. "And you can't simply sign over the percentage of the company, of course. That would be criminally stupid."

Susannah was grateful for the sunglasses she was wearing, so the tears that threatened to spill down her cheeks were not visible. "But the worst of it is, I sort of accused him of lying about the whole thing."

"Do you really think he'd lie about it?"

"Well, what am I *supposed* to think?" Susannah exploded in frustration. "I've been through almost all of Dad's stuff at the office, and there hasn't been even so much as a hint of anything like such an agreement! If Adam's telling the truth, why wasn't it mentioned in the will? Am I supposed to think that Dad's the liar, and that Adam is telling the truth? It's beginning to look as if one of them is—or was—lying."

"I don't know if this has any bearing, honey," Julia said kindly, "but that will was several years old. Josh probably should have updated it, but you know how he was about taking care of personal business."

"Yes, I know."

They were silent for most of the remainder of the drive to the job site. In Azusa they turned off the freeway onto the state highway, which wound up into the canyon, Julia exclaiming frequently over the wild, lush beauty that surrounded them.

The long, wet winter had done its work well, Susannah noted appreciatively. The mountainsides were covered with lush, green brush, and wildflowers grew in profusion. The scrubby little black oak trees that dotted the slopes had never appeared so green and healthy; everywhere the eye looked it was greeted by natural splendor.

Soon, though, if the heat wave continued, the brush would be parched and dry, and the tough little scrub oaks would lose most of their foliage under the blazing assault of the sun and the harsh, dry Santa Ana winds that blew frequently down these canyons. When that happened, the danger of forest fires would be high, and the park service would close the highways leading up into the mountains to the general public. Susannah muttered a silent prayer for one more rainstorm before summer set in with a vengeance.

"It's just beautiful up here," Julia exclaimed as they

drove past the first of the series of dams that trapped the San Gabriel River, preserving the water for future usage. "I'm so glad I came with you!"

A few minutes later the job site came into view on the right side of the highway—a vivid yellow ochre and burnt sienna scar on the canyon floor that looked jarringly out of place amid the natural surroundings. From up here on the road the conveyor belt looked like a straight, black ribbon bisecting the canyon floor right down the middle, and the yellow bulldozers and loaders parked nearby resembled children's toys. Susannah slowed the Corvette, turning off the blacktop highway onto the dirt road, which gave access to the job site, coming to a halt at a newly installed gate, before which a security guard was standing with a clipboard in his hand.

"Name and nature of business?" he asked briskly, bending down and peering into the car through mirrored sunglasses.

"I'm Susannah Lockwood, the owner of this company. This is my stepmother. I'm up here to inspect the damage. Can you tell me where I need to go?"

"Uh-huh. Mind if I see some identification?"

She took her wallet out of her purse and displayed her driver's license. The guard copied down some information on his clipboard, then touched the brim of his hat.

"Okay, Miss Lockwood, you can drive on. The damaged rig is down at the number one grizzly. You'll find Mr. McBride and the others already down there."

Susannah put the car in gear, then hesitated with her foot on the clutch. "How long have you been signing visitors on and off the job site?"

"It's standard procedure to stop noncompany vehicles on weekends," the guard replied. "I can guarantee that nobody but Lockwood personnel has been on this job site during the week, though." Nodding firmly, the guard walked over and swung the gate wide, and Susannah let the clutch out, driving on through.

She drove down the length of the conveyor, heading

toward the number one grizzly, lost in thought. If the security guard had been telling the truth, that meant that the sabotage had to have been an inside job—something they had feared all along. And that meant that it would be all that much harder to stop, she realized with a sinking sensation.

"I'm really impressed, Susie," Julia said, interrupting her chain of thought. "This all seems like quite an engineering feat to me."

"It was the most logical method," she replied distractedly, slowing down as the grizzly came into view. A cluster of private and company vehicles were parked nearby, among which she spotted Adam's pickup truck. Her heartbeat quickened at the prospect of seeing him, even after their quarrel. Several men were grouped around the big rubber-tired Caterpillar loader, watching while Bill Fredrickson and one of his mechanics scrambled around on top of it with tools in their hands.

She parked behind Adam's pickup and got out, followed by Julia. They walked over to the group of men gathered around the loader. Susannah spotted Adam a few yards away, talking with a tall man she'd never met and a uniformed security guard.

"Why, hello, Julia. Hi, Susannah." Ralph Whitman tipped his yellow hard hat and beamed at them. "Out slumming?"

"Hi, Ralph. How does it look?" Susannah asked.

"Looks like maybe we got lucky this time," Fredrickson called down to her from on top of the loader. "The engine hasn't been damaged, thanks to the guards."

"What happened?" Susannah shaded her eyes, squinting up at Fredrickson against the direct glare of the sun over his shoulder.

"Better talk to Adam," Fredrickson replied brusquely. He gestured at one of the men on the ground. "Get that fifty-gallon drum over here, Mike!"

Susannah left Julia chatting with Ralph Whitman, walking over to where Adam was talking with the two strangers. Adam turned around as she approached, his pale-blue eyes glowing with warmth for an instant, and then his mouth flattened into a straight line and his eyes became cool and remote. Last night's quarrel was fresh in his mind, too, she realized with a twinge of guilt.

"Susannah, you haven't met our night foreman, have you?" he asked, his voice crisp and businesslike. When she shook her head, he indicated the tall, rawboned man in his midfifties. "Susannah Lockwood, Highpockets Schmidt."

"A pleasure, Miss Lockwood," Highpockets murmured, bowing over her hand with a courtliness that surprised her. From what she'd heard about Highpockets Schmidt, she had expected a squat, muscular, cigar-chewing brute of a man, but this man seemed as gentle as her father had been. Still, she remembered with a smile, even Josh was capable of barking reprimands at lazy or inept workmen, so Highpockets was probably just as tough as his reputation indicated.

"And this is Tom Wilkinson, the chief security guard on the site," Adam continued.

"Pleased," Wilkinson, a stocky, dark-haired man appearing to be in his late twenties, said. "I was just telling Mr. McBride what happened last night."

"Maybe you'd better start back at the beginning, Tom," Highpockets suggested. "Since this is the lady who signs our paychecks, she's more than entitled to know what happened."

Wilkinson nodded, his eyes widening in surprise. "Well, like I was saying, I was making my rounds about midnight or a little after when I noticed this company pickup parked here by the grizzly, and some guy wearing a hard hat up on the loader. I didn't think too much of it at the time. I figured it was just one of the oilers or something—"

"The lube crew works Saturday nights," Adam interjected for her benefit. "They change the oil and filters in all the rigs and refuel them while they're shut down for the weekend."

"Yeah, right," Wilkinson went on when Adam finished. "I figured he was with the lube crew. I put the spotlight on him for a second, and he just smiled and waved, so I went on with my rounds. A few minutes later I caught up with the lube truck and asked the boys about this dude, and they didn't know what I was talking about. They said there was just the two of them on the job, and that was all that was supposed to be here." He paused dramatically, pulling out a cigarette and lighting it before continuing. "Well, I hightailed it back down here, but the guy was gone. I hustled back to the gate, and Jonesy, the night gate guard, told me a company pickup had just left, heading back down the mountain like a bat outta hell."

"I see." Susannah thought for a moment, then asked, "Is that when you called Adam?"

"No, ma'am. See, I didn't know anything was wrong yet. I had my suspicions, but all I really saw was a company pickup and a guy with a hard hat on, right? So I had the oilers come down and take a look."

"They found some spilled sugar around the fuel cap," Adam put in grimly. "That's when they called me."

"A darned good thing they did," Susannah remarked. "And thank goodness the sugar didn't get into the engine this time."

"Bill says they can drain the contaminated fuel and rinse the tank with solvent," Highpockets said. "And no harm done."

Susannah smiled at him, then asked Wilkinson, "Can you describe the man you saw?"

"Sure. He looked about fifty, fifty-five. He was sitting down up there when I saw him, so I got no way of estimating his height, but he was skinny, wiry looking, and wore glasses . . . had a hard hat on, so I don't know what color his hair was."

"Hell," Adam remarked wryly, "that description fits about half the men on the job."

"But half the men on the job wouldn't have access to a company truck," Susannah pointed out.

"We've got a lot of pickups, Susannah," Adam said

thoughtfully. "Each foreman drives one, on each of the jobs in progress, and the belt runners drive them . . ." He took off his hard hat and wiped the sweat from his forehead, frowning. "And there's always two or three down at the main yard, for the guys in the shop and office to use. It's not going to be easy to eliminate every one, Susannah."

"You can eliminate the belt runners' pickups right up front," Wilkinson pointed out. "Their pickups were parked up at the trailer the whole time. I checked."

"And I think you can eliminate me," Highpockets chimed in with a gruff little laugh. "The guards called me at home as soon as they called you. Since I live an hour from the job, I wouldn't have had time to even get home before they called."

Adam nodded, and Susannah said, "Whoever this guy is, he's as bold as brass, and he'd have gotten away with it if Wilkinson hadn't been suspicious enough to have the oilers check the loader out before servicing it. Monday morning, we'd have had another frozen diesel engine to deal with."

"That's right." Adam looked soberly at Wilkinson. "We owe you a vote of thanks."

"I was just doing my job, that's all," Wilkinson replied, flushing with pleasure. "If there's nothing else?"

"One more thing," Susannah added as he started to turn away, "would you recognize this guy if you saw him again?"

"Sure, I think so. Do you have somebody in mind?"

She hesitated, then said, "No, not really. Thanks again."

They looked after him as he climbed into the compact Ford pickup with the gold Special Security Systems shields emblazoned on the doors. As he waved and drove back up the belt line, Highpockets cleared his throat and spoke to Susannah.

"He can say what he wants, but I still say we *owe* that fella. Plenty of guys would've been taken in by that routine of company truck and hard hat. Took some smarts for him to do what he did."

"I agree." Adam glanced sheepishly at Susannah. "I guess I owe you an apology for my crack about the guards, don't I?"

She smiled, understanding that he was apologizing at least in part for the harsh words they'd exchanged last night. "I'll call Mr. Bushnell and recommend a bonus for him," she said. "He sure saved us a pile of money."

Highpockets nodded and glanced at his watch. "If there's nothing else, Adam, I'll get going. I still have a few hours of my day off left, and I'd like to enjoy them." He doffed his hard hat and smiled at Susannah. "Miss Lockwood, it was a pleasure. Hope to see you again."

"Same here, Highpockets," she returned, smiling warmly. "Keep up the good work."

With Highpocket's departure they were alone. Susannah looked over at the group clustered around the loader. Fredrickson had connected a length of rubber hose to the bottom of the fuel tank and was evidently draining the sugared diesel fuel into the large drum on the ground. Julia was still talking with Ralph Whitman, who was closely watching the activity on the loader.

When the silence had lasted long enough to become uncomfortable, Susannah began quietly, "Adam, last night I said—"

"I know what you said last night," he interrupted, his deep voice edged with anger, "and I'd just as soon not hear it again." He paused and drew a deep, ragged breath, refusing to look at her. "I appreciate what you want to do for Sheila, if you're still interested in her, that is, but I think it's best if you and I just stay the hell away from each other, except where the job demands it."

"Of course I still want to help Sheila!" she exclaimed, puzzled and hurt by his abruptness.

"Fine. I'll talk to her about the dancing lessons this afternoon. I'll tell Mrs. Lopez to call you tomorrow if she's interested. In the meantime," he said mockingly, tipping his hard hat in unconscious imitation of

Highpockets, "I think I should give notice that I'm going to accept that job with Beck and Gray. I'll work until September first, then I'll close up the house, and Sheila and I'll be leaving the country."

"Adam, wait!" she protested as he turned on his heels and began to stride away. "I want to talk to you!"

"Talk?" he demanded, turning back with his eyes blazing. "Every time you and I *talk*, we end up hurting each other. You have a cruel tongue, lady," he said softly, shaking his head, "and I just can't compete with you. I've had enough pain in my life already without you adding to it. No," he finished flatly, "any further talking between you and I will be over the phone and will concern this job or my daughter. Nothing else."

Blinded by tears of grief and frustration, she heard, rather than saw, the sound of his pickup roaring away from the job site. She turned her back on the group of people at the loader, staring at the canyon wall a hundred yards away, gulping back the sobs that filled her throat until she had regained control of herself. After taking several deep breaths, she trudged wearily back over to her car. She sat down in the driver's seat and leaned her head back on the rest, closing her eyes. A moment later she heard Julia come over and get into the car.

"Are you okay?" Julia inquired after a moment.

"I'm just fine," Susannah muttered. "Let's get out of here." She switched on the engine and turned the car around, then drove toward the gate, shifting through the gears with a savage disregard for the clutch and transmission.

Julia sat in silence until they were halfway down the canyon, glancing over at Susannah every few seconds with concern in her eyes. Finally, she asked, "I don't suppose you're hungry?"

Susannah looked over at her stepmother and managed a twisted smile. "Well, I did promise you lunch, didn't I?"

"If you're not in the mood, though . . ."

"I've got to eat," Susannah said, sighing. "All I've had since last night is a couple of cups of coffee."

"Well, there's this place Josh took me a couple of times," Julia said tentatively, "where they serve a buffet lunch on Sundays. There's a group called the Hot Pralines that play there. They sing the old stuff and have a really mellow, swinging sound. What do you think?"

Susannah smiled with false brightness. "Sounds like just the ticket. How do we get there?"

"It's called The Canyon Lodge," Julia replied with more enthusiasm, "and it's just a block off the highway, right after we get into town."

Susannah drove the winding canyon road with mechanical precision, trying to dispel the image of Adam's angry, resentful glare that kept rising up in her mind. She realized what had created such deep anger: it was her remark about the fire that killed his wife and destroyed his home. He could probably absorb just about anything else—their arguments to date had demonstrated that—but her cruel barb about him having to deny it so vehemently had finally pierced his armor, inflicting a wound that wouldn't heal easily, if ever. She could have bitten her tongue off when she realized what she'd said, but the words had been spoken, had hung in the air between them like smoke from the barrel of a gun that had just been fired, and there was no taking them back. *Adam's right,* she admitted inwardly, *I do have a cruel tongue.* A cruel tongue that had created a rift between them that threatened to open into a gap of misunderstanding that could never be crossed . . .

"You turn left at the next street," Julia said.

The parking lot in front of The Canyon Lodge was filled, with only a few empty spaces remaining. Susannah parked and got out of the car, taking a deep breath, trying to force her mood to improve, wondering if she'd ever feel hungry again.

Her mood lifted slightly the moment they entered the large, informal restaurant and heard the music, a soft, swinging rendition of "Slow Poke," the four male voices blending with the three guitars and the bass in a way that was almost anachronistic in the age of rock and heavy metal.

"Nice, huh?" Julia smiled as the hostess led them to a table for two near a large circular fireplace in the center of the room.

"Very nice," Susannah agreed as they sat down and picked up the menus.

"Would you ladies like a drink before ordering?" the hostess asked cheerfully. "Margaritas are the special today."

"Iced tea for me," Susannah replied.

"I think I'll try one of the margaritas," Julia said.

On the stage the band segued into a soothing version of "Tangerine." Susannah tilted her head, listening closely for a moment. Julia was right. *This place is just what I need,* she thought.

"They're good, aren't they?" Julia remarked, smiling at the expression on Susannah's face. "Josh used to love to come here. I don't know why we didn't come more often. Too busy, I suppose . . ."

"Here we are, ladies. Are you ready to order now, or would you like a few more minutes?"

"We'll wait a bit longer," Susannah answered. She felt much better, but her appetite hadn't yet returned.

"You might as well order something," Julia said wryly, as the waitress walked away. "If you had another fight with Adam, you're not going to feel really hungry for hours. I speak from experience, kid."

Susannah glanced through the menu, then closed it and pushed it away. "I'll have a hamburger, I guess."

Julia looked at her for a moment with compassion in her eyes. "Want to talk about it?" she asked quietly.

Susannah shook her head quickly. "I don't even want to *think* about it yet."

"That bad, eh?" Julia rummaged in her purse for a cigarette and her lighter. As she exhaled a cloud of blue smoke, she studied her stepdaughter through narrowed eyes. "This is probably the wrong time to ask, but have you found out anything about—"

"About Dad's death?" Susannah supplied. "I've been through almost every scrap of paper he left at the office, and I haven't found a thing." She took a sip of her tea, a disconsolate expression on her face. "Sometimes I think I'm just spinning my wheels, Julia. Maybe the best thing for me to do would be to just sell the company, like everybody wanted me to do, and go somewhere far away."

Julia patted her hand. "Things will look better to you in a few days. You'll see."

Susannah nodded, though she didn't have much hope that Julia was right. The waitress arrived a moment later and took their orders. While they waited for the food to arrive, they sat quietly, listening to the music.

"Here you are!" the waitress chirped brightly, placing their food on the table. "Enjoy your meal."

"Thank you." The hamburger was tasteless, at least in Susannah's present state of mind, but she managed to get most of it down, ignoring Julia's enthusiastic comments about her order of teriyaki chicken. When they were finished, Susannah grabbed the check and stood up.

"Ready?"

"I suppose," Julia shrugged. "I *was* going to have another margarita, but if you're in a hurry . . ."

Ten minutes later they were on the freeway, heading back toward Upland. Julia was silent for most of the ride, glancing over at Susannah every few seconds as if she wanted to say something, then closing her mouth as if she'd changed her mind at the last possible moment. When they stopped in front of her house in Upland, she sat in the passenger seat for several seconds, a troubled expression on her face.

"Come in for a minute," she said at last. "I have something for you."

"Thanks anyway, but I really have to go. I've got my laundry to do, and—"

"I wouldn't ask if it wasn't important!" Julia interrupted. "Come in, just for a minute."

As she followed her stepmother into the house, Susannah wondered what was so important that it couldn't have waited another day or two. She was in no mood for a lecture about the foolishness of prying into the circumstances of Josh's death, and from the expression on Julia's face, that was what she expected. Julia led her into the family room.

"Fix yourself a drink, if you want one," she directed. "I'll be right with you."

Susannah sat down, fidgeting impatiently. Whatever was on Julia's mind, she hoped it wouldn't take much time.

"I found this in Josh's closet the other day," Julia began, carrying a small steel lockbox into the room. She placed it on the table and stepped back with the air of having rid herself of something dangerous. "I finally got up enough nerve to go through his clothes for the Salvation Army and found it on the floor, pushed up against the back wall."

Susannah looked at the box. It was about a foot square and four inches deep, with a top that lifted away to expose the contents. She tugged on the small handle.

"Is there a key?"

"If there was, I don't know what happened to it. It never turned up around here. But you could pop that thing open with a butter knife."

"Why haven't you opened it, Julia?"

Nervously, Julia lit a cigarette. "Scared, I guess. I started to a couple of times, but I guess I was afraid of what I might find."

"Julia," Susannah said feelingly, "Dad worshipped you! You have nothing to fear." She was tempted to mention her conversation with Dr. Robinson but didn't. Instead she stood up and hugged Julia. Julia clung to her for a moment, then pushed her away.

"Just get it out of here, that's all I ask. Maybe there's

something in there that'll help you find out what you need to know. In any case I only want to be rid of it."

"Well . . . all right, then." Susannah picked up the box, hesitating, worried about Julia's state of mind. "If there's anything I—"

"Please. Just take it away."

As she drove toward home, she kept glancing down at the steel box on the passenger seat, eager to explore its contents. She felt intuitively that the contents of the box would provide the answers to at least some of the questions that had been taunting her for so long.

As she came up onto her doorstep, the phone began ringing inside. Rattled, it was several seconds before she managed to open the door, then she ran over and snatched it from its cradle, afraid that the caller might have given up. She was hoping it was Adam, and that he was calling to say he'd reconsidered and wanted to see her.

"Hello?" she said breathlessly.

"Is this Susannah Lockwood?" an unfamiliar voice asked.

"Yes, it is. Who's calling, please?"

"This is Sergeant Milhouse of the Upland Police Department. I've been trying to reach you all day. You—"

"Sorry, I've been out on business," she interrupted.

"Uh-huh. You *are* the present owner of Lockwood Construction Company?" When she confirmed this, Sergeant Milhouse continued. "A pickup truck registered to your company was involved in an injury accident this morning at approximately one forty-five A.M."

"An injury accident? Who was the driver?"

"Well, it wasn't the driver who was injured," Sergeant Milhouse stated flatly. "As a matter of fact he's in a detention cell right now, waiting for somebody to post his bail. He's been charged with felony drunk driving, Miss Lockwood. He badly injured a pedestrian, and your employee is in some pretty serious trouble."

"Who *was* the driver?" Susannah demanded. From the time of the accident it seemed possible that the driver of the pickup could be the man who had attempted the sabotage on the canyon job.

"A Mr. Glen Vincent," the sergeant replied. "What puzzles me, in view of the fact that he was driving one of your pickups, is his insistence that we *not* call you. Naturally, we have to notify the registered owner of the vehicle involved . . . Vincent *is* one of your employees, isn't he? He had a set of keys to your yard, and he was wearing a Lockwood and Sons hard hat at the time of the accident."

"He's a *former* employee, officer." Susannah paused for a moment, frowning in concentration. "And you just *might* be adding vehicle theft to the charges against Mr. Vincent before it's all over."

She felt a savage burst of exultation as she replaced the receiver. *At least one of my problems appears to be solved,* she thought, *because if Glen Vincent isn't the man behind the sabotage on the canyon job, then I'm Granny Goose!* Evidently, losing his bid to take over the company, followed so closely by his ignominious dismissal, had unhinged him, driving him to commit the acts of vandalism against the company. She shook her head slowly. Vincent's vindictiveness had carried him over the edge this time.

She turned her attention to the steel lockbox at last, hoping to find the solution to another set of problems inside.

CHAPTER TEN

"Your father was suffering from terminal cancer, Miss Lockwood." Dr. Paul Cranston closed the manila folder and looked across the polished wooden desk at Susannah with compassion in his eyes.

"Thank you, doctor," she said feelingly. "You don't know what a relief this is for me, and will be for my stepmother."

Dr. Cranston, a tall, slender man in his midforties, stood up and leaned against the edge of his desk, shaking his head slowly. "I can't find it in my heart to condemn him for what he did, though I might have chosen a different method . . . Josh was facing a slow, painful, and unhappily, inevitable death. In a way it took a lot of courage to do what he did."

"Courage?" Susannah cocked her head quizzically. "Most people would probably say he took the coward's way out."

"You and your stepmother would have had to watch him literally waste away, Miss Lockwood." Dr. Cranston's eyes were bleak as he looked at her. "One of my patients, a big fellow like your father, weighed eighty-one pounds when he finally succumbed, railing against his fate with his last breath. You and your stepmother are fortunate. You can remember him the way he was at his best."

"What you say makes a lot of sense, doctor," she admitted, getting to her feet and extending her hand. The doctor took her hand and held it firmly for an instant. "Thanks very much for seeing me on such short notice."

The physician waved her thanks away, patting her on the shoulder as he opened the door of his office for her. "I liked your father, Miss Lockwood, and I'm glad I was able to set your mind at ease."

As she left the office, Susannah thought back to Sunday night, when she had finally managed to force open the locked steel box with the aid of a heavy screwdriver. Finding Dr. C was so easy it was almost anticlimactic, after all her previous efforts.

Among the papers and personal items in the box, Susannah found a file of canceled checks from a private checking account, one of which Julia apparently had had no knowledge. She soon found a number of checks made out to Dr. Paul Cranston, the dates coinciding with the appointments in the battered date book she'd found so many weeks ago. From that point it was simply a matter of calling Cranston's office and making an appointment. Ironically, she recalled as she got into her car and started the engine, Dr. Cranston's office was located in the same medical block as Dr. Robinson's office, and she couldn't help contrasting the helpful, friendly attitude of Dr. Cranston's staff to the dragon who worked for Robinson.

She drove toward the dance studio where Julia worked with the windows on her car cranked wide open, the blast of summer air that whipped through the interior providing little relief from the relentless heat. This was the tenth consecutive day on which the temperature had soared into the nineties, even though it was not yet July. The summer was proving to be a record-setting scorcher.

She parked in front of the dance studio, looking through the plate glass windows at the row of small children going through a series of dance steps. On one side of the room a smiling woman played an upright piano; in front of the children, Julia, dressed in black leotards that displayed her still-excellent figure to good advantage, led the children through their practice.

Walking into the studio, Susannah stood quietly with

the group of parents in the spectator area, watching with a smile as Julia worked with the children. She was looking forward to attending sessions such as this with Sheila, beginning next week.

Mrs. Lopez, Adam's housekeeper and baby-sitter, had called her on Monday evening, informing her that Sheila was enthusiastic about taking dance lessons. Adam had given permission and would send a check to the studio, providing Susannah was still willing to provide transportation back and forth to the lessons.

"She can't wait, Miss Lockwood," Mrs. Lopez enthused, a smile in her voice. "It's so good to see her acting like a little girl about something!"

"Oh, that's terrific, Mrs. Lopez."

"Just let me know what time you'll be picking her up, if it's before five in the afternoon, and I'll tell Adam. After five he's usually home."

"I see. I'll try and arrange the lessons to begin earlier in the afternoon, so she can be home with her father in the evenings. They need the time together."

"Of course. So sad," Mrs. Lopez said, "a man like him, living alone with just his little girl . . ."

Susannah came back to the present as Julia caught her eye, smiled, and mouthed, "Just a minute." As the piano player finished with a flourish of chords, Julia laughed and clapped her hands.

"Wonderful, kids! You all did very well, and we're proud of you. See you all on Friday afternoon."

The tots began trooping over to their waiting parents, wearing self-important expressions on their faces as they moved in their tiny dance costumes. Most of the children were girls of four or five, but Susannah noticed a scattering of boys sprinkled among them, capering boisterously in contrast to the dignified behavior of the girls.

"What's the occasion, kiddo?" Julia wiped her face with a towel, smiling and nodding at the parents as they took charge of their children and gradually filtered out of the studio.

"Can we talk a minute, Julia? I've got some news about Dad."

"Listen," Julia replied wearily, compressing her lips into a flat, angry line. "I thought I told you—"

"Julia, listen to me." Susannah laid a hand on her stepmother's arm, looking imploringly at her. "I know why Dad did it, and it's nothing to do with you or me. He was suffering from a very painful form of terminal cancer."

"Cancer?" Julia repeated faintly. She looked away for a moment, and when she turned back to face Susannah her eyes shone with tears. "Dammit, why couldn't he have acted like a man and told me about it?"

Susannah looked around at the rapidly emptying studio. The piano player was gathering her sheet music and stuffing it into the bench, glancing curiously over at them. Susannah led Julia into the office, where they would have more privacy.

"He didn't even *hint* that anything was wrong!" Julia raged. "Damn him."

"I know, Julia, I know," Susannah soothed. "And the only thing I can think of is that Dad probably didn't want to involve you in what amounts to a fraud."

"Fraud? What are you talking about?" Julia demanded, staring incredulously.

"The double indemnity on his insurance policies." Susannah stared at her stepmother for a moment, frowning. "Don't you see? He had to die in an accident. Come to think of it, that's probably why he didn't leave any explanation of the peculiar bid on the canyon job. He couldn't let *anybody* know what he was planning, or the insurance investigators would have found out."

"The money? Who cares about the money!" Julia wiped her eyes with her hands as the tears coursed down her cheeks. "I'd rather have had my husband for another few months than all the money in the world. I feel cheated, Susie! It was my place to be with him. A husband shouldn't die alone when he has a wife who loves him!"

"I know, I know. But if you'd talked to the doctor, you might not feel so betrayed, Julia. Dad spared you and I the misery of watching an agonizing death . . . perhaps we should just leave it at that."

After a moment Julia nodded, a softer look coming into her eyes. "Damn him," she said with a sad, twisted little smile. "It's just like him, you know? Spare the little woman . . ." She drew a long, ragged breath, looking down at the floor. "I've felt so terribly, terribly *guilty!*"

Susannah just nodded, and Julia pulled her into her arms, hugging her almost painfully tight. When they parted, she was wearing a smile, and her eyes looked calmer and more serene than they had in months.

"Thanks, kid," she said huskily. "Maybe I'll be able to sleep without nightmares tonight. I'm sorry I gave you such a hard time about what you were doing."

"Forget it. You weren't so bad." Susannah hesitated a moment, then changed the subject. "Hey, Adam's daughter will be signing up for the dance lessons. I'd prefer an afternoon session, if there's an opening."

"I'll check the book, but I'm almost positive there's an opening. I'll call you if I'm wrong."

"Fine." Susannah stepped over and opened the door of the office, smiling back at Julia. "I'll see you soon."

"Susie, how *is* Adam?" Julia took a step closer, a hopeful expression on her face. "Have you two patched up your quarrel?"

"No. I guess we won't be getting over this one." Susannah shook her head. "He's given his notice, Julia. He'll be leaving the country in September to take a job in South America."

"Ah, gee, honey," Julia said softly, "I'm so sorry."

"Well, I guess you can't have everything," Susannah replied with a lightness she was far from feeling. Quickly she left the studio and got into the Corvette.

When she arrived back at her condo, Susannah put on a Benny Goodman tape, watered her parched houseplants, then began preparing a light supper, humming along with the clarinet.

You can't have everything . . .

She blinked away the hot sting of tears, trying to swallow the bitter lump in her throat as she tore up lettuce for a salad. If only the steel box had contained a copy of the purported agreement between Josh and Adam, perhaps it would have been possible to salvage her relationship with Adam. However, aside from the check file and a few personal items, the box had contained nothing of interest. The agreement, if indeed it had ever existed, remained as elusive as ever.

The next several weeks passed with alarming swiftness as the summer continued and Adam's remaining days with Lockwood and Sons grew fewer and fewer. The canyon job, the shining jewel in the Lockwood crown, proceeded ahead of schedule, almost running itself. If it continued this way, Susannah had remarked to Fred Ward one afternoon while they were reviewing production figures together, the canyon job would bring in a record-setting profit for the company when completed.

"And it's to your credit, lady," Fred had said fondly . . .

Susannah spent her days engrossed in her work, planning future jobs with Fred, consulting frequently with the superintendents and foremen on various other jobs, and overseeing the general operation of the company. Adam rarely called to consult her, but in the case of his job, no consultations were necessary.

When Sheila's dance lessons had begun, Susannah had hoped to see Adam occasionally, but he had apparently arranged his schedule so as to avoid seeing her when she picked up or delivered the child. Mrs. Lopez was the only adult she encountered at his house, and the housekeeper was singularly unforthcoming with news or gossip about her employer.

Still, she enjoyed the time she spent with Sheila. It was like watching the emergence of a butterfly from its chrysalis, the way she blossomed in the presence of the other children. She lost none of her unusual maturity around adults, but she was quickly learning to laugh and play, interacting with children her age in a very satisfactory way.

"I haven't seen your daddy in a long time," Susannah wistfully remarked when she picked up Sheila one afternoon for her lesson. "How has he been?"

"Fine." Sheila's face wrinkled in an almost comical scowl as she clutched the tote bag containing her towel and leotards against her chest. "But he's so *grouchy* all the time." She looked solemnly up at Susannah. "I wish you would come over and have supper with us again. He was so happy when you were there."

"I'd like that, honey," Susannah said, quickly averting her face, pretending to concentrate on the traffic, "but I'm afraid that isn't going to happen."

"I guess not," Sheila admitted, plucking at a loose thread on the fabric of her tote bag. She shot Susannah a glance of understanding out of proportion to her years. "We're going to South America in September anyway, when I'm four, so it doesn't matter. Daddy'll probably be happy when we go there."

"I hope so, honey. I sincerely hope so . . ."

Susannah and Julia had become closer than ever since her discovery of the reason for Josh's suicide, spending many evenings together going to movies or visiting friends. Ralph Whitman and his wife invited the two of them for dinner at least once every couple of weeks, and they had returned the favor, inviting the Whitmans to dinner at Julia's house more than once. All in all, Susannah reflected, she was living the life of a middle-aged widow, and when in late June Julia suggested a Fourth of July party, she eagerly embraced the idea.

"Why not make it a fifties party?" she suggested. "Everyone can dress up in period clothes, and we'll have nothing but music from the forties and fifties."

Julia nodded eagerly. "We can have all the key people from the company—Ralph and Anna Whitman, Fred and his wife, Ed Highsmith and Highpockets and their wives or girl friends. I'll ask Shari, from the studio." She paused, then added with studied casualness, "And Adam McBride, of course."

"Yes, of course." Susannah felt her cheeks flooding with heat in spite of her effort not to react. Just the mention of his name was enough to trigger unwanted emotions, and sometimes she thought it would be a relief when he finally left the country.

"Do you want to have it here," she asked, "or should I reserve the rec room at the condos?"

"Oh, let's have it here," Julia said. "It'll be fun, decorating the family room and patio. We'll just throw the sliding glass doors wide open and fix up the family room with a bar and table for the hors d'oeuvres. Hey," she added brightly, "what do you think about trying to hire the Hot Pralines to play for the party? I'll bet they know all the golden oldies, and that way we could dance."

Susannah smiled wistfully, closing her eyes for a moment. "Dancing under the stars on a warm summer night . . . sounds *very* romantic."

"Mmm." Julia looked at her and raised her eyebrows. "Bad idea, huh?"

"No, of course not!" Susannah replied stoutly. "Listen, don't tiptoe around my feelings, Julia. I'm not about to just bow out of life altogether, even if . . ." She shook her head firmly as her voice trailed off. "Dancing under the stars will be fun," she declared.

"Well, there's not much time, if we're going to do it," Julia pointed out. "Let's draw up a list of people to invite, and then they'll have to be called—there won't be time for cards to go out. I'll arrange for the catering and get started on the decorating if you'll take care of the calls. Fair enough?"

Everyone Susannah contacted with the idea responded enthusiastically—everyone except Adam. When she finally worked up nerve enough to call him, he was brisk and impersonal.

"Sorry," he declared flatly, "I'm not interested."

"Oh, come on," Susannah said jocularly, "consider it a

company function. After all, you'll be getting together socially with all the key personnel from the company. All the jobs are going to be shut down for the holiday, so why not relax and enjoy it?"

"Frankly, I'm not interested in the fact that you consider a 'fifties party' a company function," he said tersely, "especially in view of the fact that I'll be leaving the company soon." He paused for a few seconds, then added, "As a matter of fact, Susannah, I'm a little puzzled over why you'd even invite me in the first place, considering—"

"Julia particularly asked that you be invited," she broke in, her voice flat and impersonal, regretting the jocular tone she had taken a few minutes ago. "She and Josh have always thought a lot of you, but if you feel it would be too much of a problem to at least put in an appearance, then I'll try to explain it to her. Suit yourself, Adam."

Abruptly she hung up the phone. "Damn you," she whispered, staring angrily at the instrument. "Stubborn, arrogant, stupid fool!"

On the day of the party Susannah went to Julia's house in the afternoon to help put the finishing touches on the decorations and help set up the rented tables and chairs. She brought her dress and the wig she'd rented to get the 'fifties' look, putting them in her old room before setting to work.

By seven thirty the preparations were complete. The Japanese lanterns had been strung up over the patio and were glowing softly in the rapidly fading twilight, and the dining table in the family room had been pressed into service as the bar. The Hot Pralines had arrived and were setting up their amplifiers and music stands, and the caterers had delivered the platters of cold cuts and cheeses and relish trays that would serve as hors d'oeuvres.

"Whew," Susannah said, "I feel as tired as if we'd

already *had* the party!" She glanced at the clock. "I'm going to get dressed, Julia."

"Me, too." Julia walked over to the concrete slab behind her garage and spoke to the leader of the band, asking him to get the door if there were any early arrivals, then disappeared into the master bedroom.

Susannah showered quickly and freshened up, then put on the wide skirt she'd rented, over the several crisp, ruffled petticoats that went with it. She wore a low-necked peasant blouse and brown penny loafers with white socks and completed her costume by knotting a silk scarf around her neck. When she carefully placed the brunette wig with a long ponytail on her head and pirouetted in front of the mirror, she thought she could have stepped out of one of the pictures in her father's photo album from his college days.

"You look terrific!" Julia exclaimed when Susannah rejoined her in the family room. Susannah took one look at her stepmother and burst into delighted laughter.

"Oh, mommy dearest," she hooted, holding her sides and reeling with laughter. "No more wire hangers!"

"Not bad, eh?" Julia arched an eyebrow and struck a pose, one hand on her hip, the other touching up the Joan Crawford wig she'd rented. "How does it look, seriously?"

"You could have just stepped off the set of *Mildred Pierce,*" she said. "Seriously, it looks great. Too bad there are no door prizes."

Julia walked over to the bar and poured an ounce of whiskey into a glass, then dropped several ice cubes in it. "Have a drink," she invited, "before the guests start arriving."

A few minutes later the doorbell rang. Susannah opened the door and smiled at Fred Ward and his wife, Emma.

"I told you we'd be the first ones here," Emma scolded when they walked into the empty family room with Susannah.

"Dammit, I'm invited for eight o'clock, I *get* there at

eight o'clock," Fred grumbled testily. "Where's the booze?"

By eight thirty the party was in full swing. Everyone who had been invited, with the exception of Adam, had arrived within half an hour of the stipulated time, and several couples were swaying on the patio to the music of the Hot Pralines, the colored light from the Japanese lanterns playing across their faces. The band was a hit with the guests, most of whom were in their forties or fifties. The music the Hot Pralines were playing was the music they'd grown up with, and they responded by keeping the dance floor crowded with almost every number the band played.

Susannah was standing near the bar in the family room, watching wistfully while several couples danced to "Blueberry Hill," when Highpockets Schmidt walked up and smiled at her. He was wearing a double-breasted, pin-striped suit and had his hair greased and slicked back in a ducktail.

"I bought this thing in '49," he grinned, "so I guess it qualifies as fifties wear. And how long's it been since you saw a hand-painted tie this wide?"

"You look terrific, Highpockets," Susannah remarked, smiling, "and so does your wife."

"Yeah, but we had to rent her outfit," he admitted. "She's quite a bit younger than I am." He took a sip from the glass of beer in his hand, looking out over the patio. "This is the best idea anybody's had in a long time, kid," he said quietly. "Just what me and the old lady needed."

"Everyone seems to be enjoying themselves," Susannah returned with a trace of smugness.

"Yeah, they do." Highpockets sobered as he changed the subject. "I heard Vincent drew three years probation on the drunk driving charge. Looks like it was him all along, don't it? Hasn't been any more problems since he got busted in the company truck that night."

Susannah's smile faded. "I'm almost sorry he didn't go to jail, Highpockets. But I suppose in a way it was my fault. I'm the one who forgot to get his keys from him when I should have."

"No way, lady," Highpockets declared adamantly, shaking his head. "Guy like that, he'd have figured out some way to make trouble, keys or no keys." He paused for a moment, frowning. "Only thing I can't figure is *why?* Why'n hell did he have such a grudge against the company?"

"Julia went down and talked to him, after his wife bailed him out of jail." Highpockets looked at her attentively as she went on. "According to what Glen told her, it was all Josh's fault."

"Josh's fault?" Highpockets exclaimed. "How the hell'd he figure that?"

"Glen had the idea that he should have inherited a good percentage of the company when Dad died. He *did* spend most of his career with Dad. Who knows?" She sighed, shaking her head. "Maybe Dad *should* have been more generous with him in the will. I don't know, but frankly, considering the hell he put us all through, I don't much care. He tried to buy the company from me when I took over, concealing the fact that we'd been the successful bidders on the canyon job. When I wouldn't sell, he thought if he could make enough trouble for us, I'd change my mind. That's what he told Julia, anyway."

"Sonofabitch should rot in jail, if you ask me," Highpockets muttered.

"Maybe he's been punished enough," Susannah replied quietly. "He's a lonely, embittered old man now. The important thing is that we won't be having any more trouble with him."

"Josh should've canned him years ago," Highpockets insisted. When Susannah didn't reply, he nodded abruptly and wandered away.

Susannah turned away to refill her wineglass, and when she turned back around, she was face-to-face with Adam. He was dressed in a stiff new pair of Levis, glossy penny loafers, and a knit shirt and had unsuccessfully attempted to comb his wavy hair back into a ducktail.

"Hello there, boss," he greeted, smiling loosely. "Are you the bartender, or is he away at the moment?"

"I'll fix this one," she said, going behind the table, "but I can tell it's far from your first one of the evening. What'll it be, Adam?"

"Bourbon and soda, heavy on the bourbon." When she handed the glass to him, he looked into her eyes. "So how've you been, Susannah? World treating you all right?"

"Sure." She shrugged, trying to still the hammering of her heart as she came back from behind the table, standing close to him. He smelled strongly of alcohol, mixed with the clean sharp aromas of shaving lotion and soap. "I haven't been doing much."

"Me either," he said. "Working and sleeping, about it."

"Looking forward to your new job?"

He shrugged. "A job's a job."

"I'm glad you came, Adam. It'll mean a lot to Julia."

"Good old gal, Julia," he agreed.

"She thinks a lot of you."

"Oh, sure," he flipped dryly. "Bet she wouldn't if she knew I tried to take part of the company away from you." He tossed off half his drink, wincing at the bite of the alcohol.

"She knows about the agreement," Susannah replied defiantly. "The one I could never find."

"Yeah? Well, to hell with it. Easy come, easy go." His lips twisted as he shook his head. "Should've never mentioned the damn thing to you." He raised his glass and drained it. Susannah winced. She'd mixed the drink as he had requested: heavy on the bourbon.

"Adam, let's not go on this way," she said softly, placing her hand on his arm, giving an inadvertent little shiver at the touch of his warm, firm muscle. "I tried to apologize to you—"

"Apologize?" He reached for the bourbon bottle and poured more whiskey into his glass. "That's what we *do*, you and I. First we hurt each other, then we apologize

. . . keeps everybody all stirred up that way." He gave a snort of laughter as he took a pull at his drink. "Ain't that the truth, Susie?"

"Adam, don't you think you've had enough?"

He winked at her as he tipped his glass again. "I'll decide when I've had enough, Susie." He raised the glass and squinted at it. "I figure one more of these should do the trick for me."

"I don't think I want to stand here and watch you do this to yourself. If you ever want to talk when you're sober, call me."

Adam seized her by the arm as she started to turn away, spinning her around to face him. "We'll talk now, lady, if you don't mind. I'm here at your invitation, so don't walk off on me."

"Fine, then," she snapped, her blue eyes glinting with anger. "What do we talk about?"

"Come over here." He led her out onto the patio, and they wended their way through the dancers out onto the grass of the backyard. When they were standing under a tree, out of the flickering colored light from the Japanese lanterns, he released her arm.

"I guess it's confession time, Susie. See, I haven't been completely honest with you, and that crack of yours a few weeks ago has really made me think." He looked back at the patio for a few seconds, his eyes reflecting the glint of the lanterns, the leaves of the tree scattering shadows across the planes of his face. "It's just possible that the fire *was* my fault, Susie."

"Oh, no, Adam," she said, staring at him.

"Oh, yes, Adam," he mimicked, but she could see the pain in his eyes, giving the lie to the mockery in his voice. "Let me tell you a little story about a man who was too much in love with his job, boss lady . . .

"I was working on a job for your dad, way out near Barstow. We were working twelve hours a day, six days a week. I was the labor foreman then, so they were hard hours." Shaking his head at the memory, he took another drink of his whiskey. She put her hand on his, trying to stop him, but he shook her off, scowling.

"Dammit, leave me alone, if you want to hear this," he warned her. She nodded, and he continued. "Well, like I was saying, long, hard hours. I'd come home every night and fall into bed like a dead man—driving the whole fifty miles every morning and every night." He paused for a moment, a tortured expression on his face, and she felt a surge of compassion for him.

"You don't have to tell me this, Adam."

"The hell I don't. I have to tell *somebody,* and who better than you?" He glared at her for a moment, weaving unsteadily, then went on. "Anyway, Ann had bought this new gas range for the trailer. The one that came with it was no good, and when I made labor foreman she went out and got us a new one. But I was too busy, too tired, to take the time and hook it up for her."

He broke off for a moment, turning away to stare into the dark while he gradually recovered control of himself. She started to reach out to him, then held back, realizing that it would be better to let him get it out.

"She finally hooked it up herself," he whispered, "while I was laying on my ass, sleeping a whole Sunday away. And she—"

"Adam, please," she said faintly, almost certain she knew what was coming, "stop."

"No way," he replied, shaking his head stubbornly. "She . . . she was so damned proud of herself for hooking that stove up, Susie. She wanted to cook my breakfast on it Monday morning, but I was in too much of a hurry to get back to the job. The damned job was more important than my wife wanting to fix my breakfast on her brand new stove." He choked back a hoarse sob, groaning, "Oh, God, if I'd only let her fix my damned breakfast, maybe she'd still be alive! The goddamned stove blew up, Susie!"

"Oh, Adam, it wasn't your fault!" She tried to pull him into her arms to comfort him, but he spun away, wild and incoherent in his misery, refusing to listen. "You were working long hours. You were tired, exhausted—nobody could have expected you to work your Sundays, too! She should have waited for you to hook it up for her!"

"Yeah?" His eyes were dark with misery when he looked at her, but he shook his head with monotonous regularity, like a metronome, ignoring whatever comfort she had been trying to offer. "Maybe so, but she didn't. It was *my* job, wasn't it? It wasn't her job, dammit—it was mine! And because I didn't do it, she . . . died." He lifted his glass, grimaced when he saw it was empty, and tossed it into the shrubbery. After turning and staring at her face for a long moment, he pushed past her and staggered toward the patio, stumbling through the crowd of dancers, ignoring those who called out greetings or protests.

"You poor, poor guy," she whispered, watching sadly as he thrust his way through the family room, heading toward the front door. "No wonder you're so terribly unhappy."

CHAPTER ELEVEN

Summer took hold with a vengeance during the weeks following the party at Julia's, bringing endless days when temperatures soared into the low hundreds. The brassy, glaring sun baked the moisture out of every living thing in southern California, drying up lawns and shrubs and bringing on water rationing in Upland for the first time in many years.

Susannah's office trailer was air-conditioned, or work would have been impossible. As it was, the air-conditioning unit made the heat in the oversized metal box barely tolerable, and she and Fran Parker replenished the moisture in their bodies by consuming copious amounts of sun tea, taking turns running to the market for sacks of ice that they kept in an ice chest.

Adam remained on the canyon job, spinning out his last days with the company in hermitlike isolation. He rarely came by the yard and never stopped at the office. If a tool or a part from the maintenance shed was required, he dispatched one of the foremen or called Bill Fredrickson. Since the night of the party he had avoided Susannah with a determination that bordered on the fanatical. If it hadn't been for the weekly personal checks he sent with Sheila to pay for her dance lessons, Susannah might have suspected he'd already left town.

During the first week in August, Susannah was sitting at her desk, signing the payroll checks for distribution on the following day, Friday, when the telephone rang.

"Yes?"

"Susannah, this is Julia. Our air-conditioning at the

studio is on the fritz, so lessons for the next few days are cancelled." Julia sighed. "We won't even be able to get a repairman until next week, can you believe it?"

"Oh, that's too bad. I'll call Mrs. Lopez so she can tell Sheila. I know she'll be disappointed."

"Can't be helped. Is it miserable there at the office?"

" 'Miserable' is the word, Julia. Even with our air conditioner on high, it hardly ever gets below eighty-five in here. There's no insulation in these walls, you know." She paused, wiping a film of sweat from her forehead. "I don't know how Dad put up with this damned place all those years. I truly don't."

"Why don't you come over to the house when you get off?" Julia suggested. "My unit will freeze your buns off."

"I've got a better idea. Why don't you come over to the condo about five? We'll spend the evening laying around the pool." She was smiling as she replaced the receiver. Julia had been much easier to get along with during these past few weeks and had provided Susannah with badly needed moral support.

She scrawled her signature across the last of the payroll checks, then gathered them up and carried them in to Fran for sorting. "Better have one of the guys run the canyon checks up right after lunch, Fran, so Ed Highsmith can get them sorted out for the night shift."

Fran nodded, and Susannah walked over to the jug of sun tea on the credenza, where she filled a large plastic tumbler. Kneeling, she took several ice cubes from the ice chest, dumping them into the tea.

"What are you doing for lunch?" Fran asked, flicking rapidly through the pile of green checks, sorting them into piles according to job locations.

"Lunch?" Susannah asked. "Who can eat in this heat?"

"I was thinking about going to Farrell's, myself," Fran said with a grin. "Maybe have a pineapple sundae."

"Hey, you might have something there," Susannah replied, brightening a bit. "I've lost nearly ten pounds since this heat wave hit, so I can afford to splurge one time. Mind some company?"

"That's why I was asking. About twelve, then?"

Nodding, Susannah carried her tumbler of iced tea back into her office, where last week's production figures awaited her inspection. Sitting down, she began going through the figures, frowning when she noticed a slight drop in production on the day shift two days last week. *Damn.* Normally she would simply call Adam and ask for an explanation, but with the tension between them, and his determined avoidance of her, she was reluctant to call. She looked back at the figures, sipping absently at her tea. Production was back up to normal on Thursday and Friday, so whatever had happened had evidently been cleared up . . .

"Fran!" she called out, grimacing. "Did you remember to pick up a package of sweetener when you went for ice?"

Fran appeared in her doorway, a guilty expression on her face. "I forgot it," she said softly. "Wait. Maybe I've got some in my desk."

"Never mind," Susannah said. "I think I saw some here in the top drawer the other day." She rolled her chair back a few inches and pulled on the drawer, but it refused to budge. "Oh, damn this thing," she muttered. "I haven't opened it for a day or two, and now it won't budge." Grasping the front of the drawer by the lip with both hands, she gave a sharp pull. Instantly the drawer shot forward, sliding all the way out on its metal rollers, spilling a load of paper clips, crumpled envelopes, toothpicks, coins, staples, and ballpoint pens all over the floor. Holding the drawer by its lip, Susannah stared, appalled, at the mess on the floor.

Fran giggled behind her hand. "But look," she said, struggling to control herself, "there *was* a pack of sweetener, so it's not a total loss."

"Terrific." Susannah placed the empty drawer on the floor and knelt, picking up its contents and putting them back into the drawer. She took the small yellow packet and placed it on the desktop near her tumbler of tea. All at once the humor of the situation struck her, and she began to giggle, softly at first, and then erupting into loud, satisfying laughter. Fran joined in, and for several moments the trailer resounded with the sound of their hilarity. At last Susannah wiped her eyes, sighing happily. "Oh, my, that was great, Fran. I haven't laughed like that since—" She broke off abruptly, staring up into the well of the desk. A folded sheet of paper was jammed into the drawer track, wedged against the drawer wall on the side of the desk.

"What is it?" Fran asked, puzzled by the sudden change of mood.

"I don't know." Moving closer, Susannah reached up and tugged the folded sheet loose. It was dusty and yellowed with age, but when she unfolded it and quickly read it, the writing was still crisp and clear, and the signatures at the bottom were unmistakable.

Joshua Lockwood and Adam McBride.

"Oh, Adam . . ." She felt the sting of tears as she refolded the paper and buttoned it into her shirt pocket. "Did you already give the canyon paychecks to somebody to deliver?"

"What?" Fran was staring at her in confusion. "Oh. Well, I called over to the shop, and Bill is going to have one of his mechanics take them up after lunch."

"Never mind. I'll deliver them myself."

"In this heat? You're going to drive up there?" Fran stared as if she'd lost her mind.

Susannah gathered her purse and car keys, then strode into Fran's office, holding out her hand. "Let me have those checks, Fran. I'll take them up right now."

"But what about lunch? Can't you wait until after lunch?"

"No, this has already waited too long," she declared, shaking her head firmly. "I've got to do it right now, before another hour goes by. It's important, maybe the most important thing I've ever done."

"Well," Fran replied, staring warily at her employer, "I'll put them in an envelope for you, then."

Ten minutes later Susannah was speeding down the freeway in her Corvette, heading toward the canyon. She had removed the top from her car several days ago, but the hot, dry air blasting through the interior provided no respite from the heat. She sped along at nearly seventy miles an hour, keeping a sharp eye out for cruising highway patrolmen.

Turning north on Highway 39, she drove through Azusa toward the canyon, barely conscious of the sparse traffic around her. She was filled with a combination of relief and remorse: relief that she had finally found the elusive copy of the agreement between Josh and Adam, and remorse that she hadn't been able to summon enough faith in Adam's character to realize he would not have lied to her. She prayed that he would understand the reasons she had been unable to accept unreservedly his version of the truth, and that he would forgive her . . .

A mile or so north of Azusa's city limits, the forestry department had erected a barricade across the highway. A tall ranger stood in the middle of the highway, waving her to a halt.

"No visitors in the canyon except for residents and business people, miss. We've got a brushfire going up there, and things could get pretty dangerous before we get it out."

"I am on business," Susannah explained, reaching for the manila envelope containing the paychecks for Adam's crews. "I'm delivering the payroll to the Lockwood job at Williams Dam."

"Do they have to get there today?" the ranger asked, scowling as she displayed one of the paychecks for him to prove she was telling the truth.

"Today's payday," she said. "Would *you* like to be the one to explain why thirty-five men on the night shift didn't get their checks on time?"

"All right, then," the ranger grumbled, shaking his

head, "but you'd think the owners of your company would be more responsible than to send a young lady like you up here under these conditions. If we have to close that road off altogether, you might not be able to get back down for a couple of days."

"I'll have to risk it," she replied. "Now, would you please move that barricade and let me by?"

Traffic in the canyon was practically nonexistent. Except for two big green forestry department trucks she met coming down, and the fire truck that passed her, its siren screaming, she had the road to herself. As she climbed into the mountains, a black pall of smoke hung in the sky, and the smell of burning wood filled the air. An occasional ash bounced off her windshield, carried down the canyon by the stiff, hot wind that was blowing. *Undoubtedly adding to the firefighters' problems*, she thought.

When the job site came into view on the right side of the highway, she was surprised to see that most of the heavy equipment had been assembled near the parking area where the men parked their personal vehicles. The crew stood around in small groups. The forestry department had shut the job down, she realized as she turned off the main highway onto the road that led to the job site.

She passed through the security gate and drove slowly toward the parking area, where Adam's big pickup was parked next to a green forestry department pickup. Adam stood a few yards away, his arms folded across his chest, frowning as he listened to the forest ranger in front of him.

He looks so tired, Susannah thought as she walked over to join the two men. The ranger spun around and stared at her in amazement.

"Damn, how'd *you* get up here, young lady?" he snapped, speaking loudly in order to be heard above the clatter of the idling diesel engines from the row of equipment parked nearby. "That highway is supposed to be closed!"

"It is closed. I brought up the paychecks for the crews."

"This is Susannah Lockwood," Adam explained. "Susannah, Tom Patek, from the state forestry department." He looked at her and raised his eyebrows, shrugging. "It's a good thing you did show up, I guess, since the state wants to requisition our equipment to fight the fire."

"Well, we'll do whatever we can to help," Susannah said quickly. "Which pieces do you need?"

"All your dozers," Patek answered. "And we'd like to have the operators as well, if they'll volunteer."

"Adam? Have you asked them?" she asked.

"Sure. Most of them will go along. But a few of the guys live down near the bottom of the canyon, and they're worried about their homes and families, so we're short several operators." He shrugged. "Patek wants to bring in state operators to run our rigs, but that'll take time, and time is what we're short on right now."

"Look at that," Patek said, turning and pointing toward the ridges that led up away from the office trailer, a quarter of a mile up the canyon from where they were standing. Susannah followed the direction of his finger and gasped. A couple of ridges behind the one where the office trailer was located, flames shot up against the horizon, and clouds of black smoke were being whipped in swirling eddies by the hot winds.

"If we don't get some firebreaks cut right away, you're going to lose your office . . . and maybe a lot of your belts. Seems to me you've got a vested interest in helping us get this fire out, Miss Lockwood."

"Of course. Adam, let's get our volunteers on those rigs right away."

"You're going to put our men on the fire line?" Adam asked, unfolding his arms and putting his hands on his hips.

"Not on the line itself," Patek replied, shaking his head. "That's a job for trained firefighters only. What we need is for your men to cut firebreaks across those hogbacks up in there, to help us keep the fire from spreading down the mountain. The danger should be minimal."

"Should be minimal," Adam repeated, snorting. "Seems to me I remember a couple of dozer operators suffocating to death a few years ago while they were cutting firebreaks in the San Bernardino Mountains."

"Well, yeah," Patek admitted, reddening slightly, "there are always risks, Adam. Dammit, how about it? Are you guys going to help out, or do I call the office and have them send up our own operators?"

"We'll help." Adam gestured toward the men who were watching them, waving his hard hat. When the men had drifted over and stood quietly, he raised his voice. "I'm asking again for volunteers. We need anybody who can skin a cat on a dozer. The rest of you guys, take off and go on home."

"I'm willing to work, but who's gonna pay me?" A burly fellow dressed in T-shirt and jeans asked.

"Frank, you're not going to work one hour without pay," Adam explained patiently. "And the state will even feed you if you work over twelve hours. Any more questions?"

"I guess not," Frank replied. "Just tell me what you want me to do, and I'll get going."

"Just hang loose a second," Adam directed, glancing over his shoulder at the row of equipment. "The rigs are being topped off with fuel right now. Mr. Patek will send us where we're needed."

"You stayin', Adam?" one of the men asked soberly.

"I was a catskinner before I made super," Adam answered with a shrug. "And they need every damn one of us they can get. I don't see any way I can walk away."

"Well, have a ball, boss," one of the men yelled, "you're gonna find out those hogbacks got a lot of bones in 'em before this day is over!" Several of the men laughed, and they wandered over to stand near their bulldozers, awaiting instructions from Patek.

"Damn, we're still short," Patek said, counting the available operators and bulldozers. "I need at least two more skinners."

"I'll run one of the D-9's," Susannah blurted.

"Good," Patek replied absently, with only a quick, surprised glance at her. "That'll help. Now—"

"Like hell you will!" Adam snapped, stepping over and seizing her by her upper arm, spinning her around to face him. "If you think I'm going to let you expose yourself to this kind of danger, you're crazy!"

"*Let* me?" She jerked out of his grasp, pointing at the flames devouring the brush on the slopes near the office trailer. "Can't you see what's happening? This is an emergency, and even if it wasn't, don't you tell me what I can and can't do!"

"Susannah, it's not your responsibility," he said reasonably. "Let us men handle this."

"Listen, Adam," she flared, "I was running a dozer long before some of these men were. Patek said they need every available hand, and I'm volunteering!"

"Running a dozer on the flatland is hardly the same as being a full-fledged catskinner, dammit! Didn't you hear what that guy said? Those hogbacks are bony—full of rocks and boulders. It's not going to be easy, peeling the brush off those ridges. Don't be an idiot, Susannah. This is man's work!"

"I'm volunteering," she insisted stubbornly, addressing herself to Patek.

"Fine with me," Patek shrugged. "Like I said—"

"Goddammit," Adam roared, "I'm not going to stand here and let you send the woman I love up there on a D-9!"

"The woman you—" Susannah started, a wild burst of happiness exploding in her chest, but Patek stepped between them, holding up his hands.

"Listen, I think I understand what's going on," he interrupted, giving them a weary smile. "And I might have the solution. Adam, I need *two* rigs up on that ridge directly behind your office, because that's where we're going to make an all-out effort to stop this thing. If we can get a thirty-foot-wide break cut on that ridge, I think we stand a good chance of containing the fire by nightfall, when the wind will die down. The way I see it, one of you could work the upper portion of the hogback, and the other one could work the side near the road, in case it came down to making a break for it."

Susannah stared at the ridge behind the office trailer, swallowing the knot of fear that rose up in her throat. The terrain was perilously steep, rock formations jutting from the cover of brush and the few scrub oaks that clung to the slope, and she knew that what she was proposing to do was a far cry from the simple bulldozing she'd been taught by Josh to do back down on the flat ground near home.

While she stared at the slope, a twin-engined airplane came roaring up the canyon at an altitude of less than five hundred feet, its engines momentarily drowning out the racket of the parked, idling equipment. The airplane made a sudden, tight turn that brought it directly over the flames. Suddenly a light-colored cloud of water and chemicals fell from the plane, briefly extinguishing a small area of the fire.

"Something, ain't it?" Patek said admiringly. "We've got two tankers working this fire. Look!"

The plane flew up the hogback, seeming to almost touch the flames as it clawed for altitude. For a moment Susannah was afraid it was going to crash, but at the last possible instant it swung wide, climbing above the ridge line. Seconds later it flew back down the canyon, passing over them with a dip of its wing.

"Let's get with it, then," Adam said brusquely. Patek had walked over to the line of waiting dozers and was gesturing broadly as he showed the men where he wanted them to work.

"Wait, Adam," Susannah called, hurrying after him, trotting in an attempt to keep up with his long strides. "I've got to tell you something!"

"It'll wait," he snapped, stopping beside one of the

huge D-9 bulldozers. "You take this rig, Susannah. Stay right on my tracks. Getting up onto that hogback isn't going to be easy, and no matter what you told Patek, I *know* you're not that much of a catskinner. Your only chance is to do exactly as I tell you. Stick with me, and I'll get you up there. Once we're up there, I think you'll be able to handle it."

"All right, Adam, but—"

"No buts," he snapped. "I'll take the rig right in front of you. Stick with me, now."

Nodding, she climbed up onto the steel treads of the huge tractor, pulling herself up by the railing that was attached to the operator's seat. She dropped into the seat, staring for a moment at the controls. It had been a long time since she'd been up on a dozer but thankfully the controls appeared to have remained the same. She gingerly grasped the throttle lever and pulled it toward her, placing her right foot on the large pedal in front of the seat. The engine roared in response to the throttle, then quickly quieted as she pressed on the decelerator pedal. Wincing, she held her hands over her ears as she raised up in the seat, watching Adam as he maneuvered his dozer out of the line of parked tractors. She'd forgotten the tremendous amount of noise generated by one of these huge machines and wished she had a pair of ear protectors to put on.

Adam's bulldozer began moving slowly up the dirt road that paralleled the belt line, heading toward the highway near the office trailer. Susannah pulled the big lever located at the right of her seat, raising the blade of the bulldozer a few inches off the ground. Moving the gear selector of the automatic transmission into forward, she began following Adam up the road, experimenting cautiously with the steering clutches, getting the feel of the big machine. When she pulled out the left-hand clutch lever, the tractor moved slowly to the left; when she pulled out the right-hand lever, the machine moved slowly to the right. Sharper turns, she remembered, required the combination of steering clutches and foot brakes.

Up ahead, Adam's dozer rolled onto the road, the steel treads screaming as if in torment as they ground against the hard surface. Susannah waited until he was across the road, then followed, wincing at the screeching din created by her own tractor's treads. When the tractor rolled onto the natural ground on the far side of the road, she almost groaned with relief at the cessation of the torturous noise. Raising up in the seat, she caught sight of Adam's dozer, standing still in a cloud of dust, and she quickly stepped on her decelerator and moved the gear selector into neutral, stopping just in time to keep from hitting the other tractor.

Adam looked back and shook his head scornfully, causing her cheeks to flush with heat. He stood up on the treads, pointing upward, and she nodded to show that she understood. He was showing her where they needed to go. When she nodded, he held up a clenched fist, the construction world's signal to "hold it." She threw her throttle all the way forward, idling her engine, then got out of the seat and stood on her treads, watching as Adam began maneuvering up the steep, rocky slope.

He proceeded slowly, having to back off once or twice when his steel treads began bouncing ineffectively on large, half-submerged boulders and start again, but gradually he established a route to the crest of the ridge. When he finally had his machine where he wanted it, he stood on the treads and gestured with his hard hat, beckoning Susannah to follow.

"Here goes nothing," she muttered to herself, pulling the throttle all the way back and putting the machine in the lowest gear for the climb. She moved forward, craning from side to side to keep the track of his dozer in view, following his route as strictly as possible. The huge diesel engine screamed as if in pain, but the tractor climbed steadily up the impossible-looking slope. Susannah was almost completely prone at times, the route was so steep. At last, after what seemed hours of struggle, she felt the nose of the dozer dip as she reached the crest of the ridge, and she stood on the left-hand brake and pulled out the left-hand steering clutch. The big machine swerved sharply until it was astride the ridge, facing down the side of the mountain. When she had it stopped and in neutral, she closed her eyes for a moment, muttering a silent prayer of thanks. When she opened her eyes, Adam was on the ground next to her tracks, motioning her down.

"What we've got to do," he yelled into her ear when she was down on the ground beside him, "is to clear this ridge of brush in a strip at least thirty feet wide. See how we're set here?" He pointed up the hill, beyond his dozer, then turned and pointed down the hill, in line with her dozer. A few hundred yards below was the paved highway, and on the right side of the ridge they were situated on, a few hundred feet below, was the office trailer. The belt line running behind the office trailer appeared as small as a matchbox from her vantage point, and she looked away quickly.

"I see," she shouted in reply. "What do I do?"

"You push *down* the hill, toward the highway. I'll go up the ridge until I come to the old forestry department firebreak and push down this way from there. That way I can sort of keep an eye on you, in case you get in trouble. Keep chopping away at it until you've got all the combustible material in a thirty-foot–wide strip pushed away."

She swallowed as she looked down toward the highway. The mountain seemed to just fall away in front of her dozer blade at a precipitous angle that terrified her.

"Adam," she said, shaking her head, "are you sure . . ."

He laughed, showing those marvelous even white teeth, and slapped her on the back. "Hell, you volunteered, didn't you?" He sobered when he saw that her fear was real. "Look, just keep your blade full of material, Susie. Keep that dozer blade *loaded*, and you aren't going anywhere you don't want to. You get to the end of your push, drop it off, and back up the hill to your starting point. Nothing to it. It just *looks* scary."

She nodded, unable to speak, and he gave her a big grin, slapping her on the back again, then turned and hurried back up to his tractor.

She climbed up into the seat of her dozer and pulled back the throttle, lowering the bulldozer blade as she moved slowly forward. The engine note changed as the blade bit into the ground, deepening with effort as the dirt curled over the edge of the blade and spilled alongside the treads as the tractor moved forward. Susannah adjusted the blade, keeping it even as the tractor crawled forward.

She gasped in fear as the nose of the dozer dipped down and the highway appeared below her, but when the tractor began to pick up speed, she simply pushed the lever controlling the height of the dozer blade forward a bit, causing it to dig deeper into the ground. The tractor instantly slowed, the dirt curling up over the edge of the blade and spilling out at the sides, creating a neat set of windrows that stretched behind her as she moved forward. She looked around, pleased, and began to relax a little.

In a way, she was astonished to discover, this was almost fun, and she had a glimmer of the reasons why many men chose to do this kind of work, year after year, until they retired. The work was exhilarating, and now the added stimulus of the dangerous fire nearby made it even more thrilling. When she reached the end of her push, where the mountain leveled off at the side of the highway, she shifted into reverse and backed rapidly up the mountain, riding on the smooth surface she had just created. *Adam's right,* she realized happily. *As long as the dozer blade's kept full, the machine's a snap to control.* Her confidence soared as she reached her starting point and began another push, and when Adam waved at her from his dozer, she flashed a wide, confident grin and waved back.

After an hour of these long, slow pushes, she was beginning to feel a little sick at her stomach. She knew it was because of the ceaseless, horrifying racket created by the tractor, but there was nothing she could do about it. The nausea would have to be tolerated until they finished what they had set out to do. However, for the first time in her life, she understood the company's safety rule that required operators of heavy equipment to wear safety equipment which included ear protection. A few months of this, she realized, and she would suffer serious hearing loss.

She glanced over at the ridge on her left. The fire seemed to be working its way voraciously toward them, devouring everything in its path, and the smell of smoke was strong enough to gag her, especially when combined with the black smoke that belched from the dozer's exhaust pipe each time the engine was under strain. The heat was almost unbearable now. The sun glared down through the haze of smoke overhead, and the engine's heat blew back over her with every push. When the heat of the forest fire was added, an inferno was created. Susannah was drenched in her own sweat, and her mouth was almost painfully dry and parched.

She was in the middle of a long push toward the highway when she noticed Patek, standing in the road in front of his forestry department pickup, gesturing wildly at her. She stopped the dozer, standing on the tracks and spreading her hands to indicate she didn't understand what he was trying to convey.

Patek leaped up and down, waving his hat as she hesitated there, then suddenly leaped into his pickup and sped away. Susannah shrugged, threw her dozer into reverse, and backed rapidly up the slope. *Perhaps Adam will know what the forest ranger's been trying to say,* she thought.

"Damn it," Adam roared when she idled back her engine and climbed down onto the ground, "didn't you see Patek?" Adam's dozer stood a few yards away where he had parked and waited for her. "Didn't you see him signaling?"

"I saw him," she shouted back, "but I couldn't make any sense of his signals! Who the hell taught him signaling, the coast guard?"

He shook his head impatiently, turning her to face back up the canyon. A hundred yards away, on the next ridge, the fire was scourging the tinder-dry vegetation, leaping from bush to bush and scrub oak to scrub oak with loud, snapping cracks that were audible even over the noise of the bulldozer engines.

"Fire storm!" he shouted, spinning her back around to face him. "That's what Patek was trying to tell you! He wanted you to bail out, get down on the road with him! You're stuck up here with me, now. It's too damned late to make the road!"

"I'd rather be with you anyway!" she shouted defiantly.

His eyes seemed to soften for an instant, then he led her across the wide bare space they had created together, toward his bulldozer. "We're going to have to dig in," he said. "I'll take my Cat and dig a ditch. I'll get it as deep as I can in the time we have, but no matter how deep it is, it's going to be our only chance."

"I don't understand, Adam. What do you mean?"

"We're going to have to go into the ditch, Susannah! If the fire storm manages to cross this break of ours, maybe it'll save our lives—if we have enough oxygen. Is there any water on your rig?"

She shook her head, not understanding.

"I've got a gallon on mine. We'll soak my shirt and put it over our heads when the time comes." He shook his head, his lips pursed grimly. "Might be enough for us to make it."

"In case we don't make it," she said, unbuttoning the flap over her shirt pocket and holding out the sheet of paper she'd discovered in her desk earlier that morning, "I want you to have this. I found it, Adam. I finally found it."

He shot her a puzzled glance, then quickly unfolded the sheet of paper and looked at it. He smiled wryly. "Hell of a time for *this*, baby. But at least you know that I wasn't lying to you all these months."

"Adam, I never—" Abruptly she closed her mouth, feeling herself blush with shame. He was right, and they both knew it. Denial would be pointless. She looked up at him, tears gleaming in her eyes. "I can only say I'm sorry."

"There you go again," he grinned, "apologizing. Forget it, Susie." Sobering, he pointed at the flames that were now at the bottom of the adjoining ravine, beginning to race up the slope toward them. It was already becoming difficult to breath, as the flames sucked the available oxygen from the heated air.

"I'm going to dig. When I stop and wave at you, you dive under my rig. Got it?"

"How about you?"

"I'll be right behind you."

All at once he wadded the sheet of paper in his hand into a ball and tossed it into the air. The hot wind caught it, toyed with it for a moment, then carried it toward the voracious flames. She stared at him in amazement, but he just nodded at her, then hurried back to his dozer.

Within a moment or two he had dug out a trench approximately fifteen feet long and four feet deep. He backed up for one more push, then his eyes suddenly widened and he stopped, waving wildly at her. She ran toward the ditch, wincing at the sound of a small scrub oak behind her exploding into fire with a loud bang.

She dove into the relatively cool dirt beneath the dozer, huddling back in the shade under its huge steel belly. An instant later Adam dived in beside her, cradling a large thermos jug. Without so much as a glance at her he tore his shirt off, ignoring the buttons. He quickly unscrewed the cap of the water jug and soaked the shirt, then ripped the shirt into two pieces.

"Cover your face with this!" he shouted above the

roaring flames that seemed to be consuming the tractor over them.

She obeyed, lying down in the curve of his body, her face concealed by the wet rag. When she felt his strong arm come up and curl slowly around her, she felt so contented she didn't care if this *was* her day to die. At long last things were right between her and the man she loved.

"—love you!" she heard Adam cry out, just as there came a tremendous crackling roar directly overhead. She gasped and felt a sharp pang in her lungs as she tried to get a breath of air. Within seconds she was spinning down, down into a black, endless vortex . . .

"Baby, are you all right?" She opened her eyes. Adam was leaning over her, his eyes shining with love. "Oh, thank God," he said when he saw her eyes open. He leaned close, kissing her with infinite tenderness. "I thought for a minute there you were gone, Susie."

"I—I guess I blacked out," she murmured, gazing up at him. His face was streaked with dirt, soot, and sweat, but she thought she'd never seen a more beautiful sight. "The fire?"

"We stopped it, Susie," he said, his white teeth starkly contrasting with the darkness of his face. "Our firebreak stopped it in its tracks. It's still burning, but at least it's contained. We did it together, baby."

"I think you and I could do just about *anything* together," she whispered softly. She sighed happily when his lips came down and covered hers for a long, tender moment. When he raised up, looking down on her with that happy glow in his eyes, she asked, "Adam, why did you throw the agreement away? It's been such an obstacle to you and me, and now that I—"

"Because it *was* such an obstacle, baby." He kissed her again, as if he couldn't get enough of the taste of her lips. "We were both wrong, Susie. You thought I was lying to you, and I, well, I thought owning a percentage of the company was important to me. I know now that having you is going to make me a damn sight happier than owning any part of Lockwood and Sons ever could. As long as you and I are right with each other, lady, then I'm right with the rest of the world."

As his mouth came down and covered hers once again, her entire being was suffused with a radiant joy, and Susannah knew that there was going to be a world of love in the life they would share.

Now you can reserve February's Candlelights *before* they're published!

- 💗 You'll have copies set aside for *you* the instant they come off press.
- 💗 You'll save yourself precious shopping time by arranging for *home delivery.*
- 💗 You'll feel proud and efficient about organizing a system that *guarantees* delivery.
- 💗 You'll avoid the disappointment of not finding *every* title you want and need.

ECSTASY SUPREMES $2.75 each

- ☐ **109 PERFECT CHARADE**, Alison Tyler.........16859-7-17
- ☐ **110 TANGLED DESTINIES**, Diana Blayne.......18509-2-17
- ☐ **111 WITH OPEN ARMS**, Kathy Alerding........19620-5-19
- ☐ **112 PARTNERS IN PERIL**, Tate McKenna......16804-X-21

ECSTASY ROMANCES $2.25 each

- ☐ **402 HEIGHTS OF DESIRE**, Molly Katz.........13615-6-19
- ☐ **403 MORE THAN SKIN DEEP**, Emily Elliott......15821-4-22
- ☐ **404 A MOMENT'S ENCHANTMENT**, Jane Atkin..15792-7-27
- ☐ **405 SEDUCED BY A STRANGER,**
   Barbara Andrews........................17635-2-57
- ☐ **406 A LOVE OF OUR OWN**, Lori Copeland.....15009-4-26
- ☐ **407 SHEER DELIGHT**, Cory Kenyon..........17596-8-62
- ☐ **408 MYSTERY LADY**, Eleanor Woods.........15997-0-12
- ☐ **409 TOGETHER IN THE NIGHT,**
   Candace McCarthy.....................18713-3-27

Dell At your local bookstore or use this handy coupon for ordering:

DELL READERS SERVICE—DEPT. B920A
P.O. BOX 1000, PINE BROOK, N.J. 07058

Please send me the above title(s). I am enclosing $_____ (please add 75¢ per copy to cover postage and handling). Send check or money order—no cash or CODs. Please allow 3-4 weeks for shipment. CANADIAN ORDERS: please submit in U.S. dollars.

Ms./Mrs./Mr_____

Address_____

City/State_____ Zip_____